To Have and to Kill

ALSO BY MARY JANE CLARK

To Have and to Kill

Mary Jane Clark

THIS BOOK IS A GIFT OF:

**FRIENDS OF THE
ANTIOCH LIBRARY**

Contra Costa County Library

HARPER LUXE

An Imprint of HarperCollinsPublishers

TO HAVE AND TO KILL. Copyright © 2011 by Mary Jane Clark. All rights reserved. Printed in the United States of America. No part of this book may be used or reproduced in any manner whatsoever without written permission except in the case of brief quotations embodied in critical articles and reviews. For information address HarperCollins Publishers, 10 East 53rd Street, New York, NY 10022.

HarperCollins books may be purchased for educational, business, or sales promotional use. For information please write: Special Markets Department, HarperCollins Publishers, 10 East 53rd Street, New York, NY 10022.

FIRST HARPERLUXE EDITION

HarperLuxe™ is a trademark of HarperCollins Publishers

Library of Congress Cataloging-in-Publication Data is available upon request.

ISBN: 978-0-06-201766-6

11 11 12 13 14   ID/RRD   10 9 8 7 6 5 4 3 2 1

For Doris Boland Behrends, my mother,
who helped me make my first cake.
And for those affected by Fragile X Syndrome.
It looks as if treatment is coming . . . soon.

To Have and to Kill

Prologue

He took her hand and squeezed it in the darkness. She held on tight as the giant dome above them filled with bright stars, flaring, exploding, and spraying the sky with colors. Listening to the explanation of what the heavenly bodies meant to mankind, the couple felt the stars rushing past them faster and faster, as if they themselves were careening through the Milky Way.

He leaned over and whispered close to her ear: "Make a wish on one of those stars."

She closed her eyes and did as she was told.

When the planetarium show was over, she started to get up from her seat. "That was fantastic," she said. "There was so much of that I didn't know. I sometimes forget that the sun is a star and that, without it, we wouldn't be alive." She gently pulled at him to get up.

"Wait a minute," he said. "Sit down again."

Usually, as one group filed out of the theater, the next filed in. He had deliberately chosen the last show of the day so they would be left unrushed and alone.

"I made a wish on one of those stars, too," he said. "I wished that you'd say yes."

She looked at him, her eyes widening.

"I'm asking you to marry me, sweetheart," he said, taking both of her hands in his. "I couldn't think of a better place to ask you than here among the stars where you belong."

She inhaled deeply, pausing for just a moment as she remembered the disturbing letter hidden at the back of her desk drawer.

His eyes searched her face. "What's wrong?" he asked.

"Nothing," she answered, trying to ignore her apprehension. "Of course I'll marry you. Yes. Yes. Yes."

Tears welling up in her eyes, she threw her arms around his neck and they held on tight to each other.

"Oh, I almost forgot," he said, pulling back and reaching into his coat pocket. He took out a little red box and opened it. Inside was a large, clear diamond solitaire set in platinum.

Her left hand trembled as she held it out and he slipped the ring on her finger. This is what she had wanted, what she had hoped would happen. But as she kissed him with joy, something else was nagging at her, leaving her feeling unsettled. For some reason, a portion of the star show they had just seen was repeating itself in her mind. What the narrator said had hit a nerve somewhere deep inside her and somehow felt like a warning.

She smiled at her fiancé but shivered as she recalled what she had just learned. Explosions ended some stars' cosmic lives. There were stars that burned hot, lived fast, and died young.

Chapter 1

Sunday, November 28 . . .
Twenty-six days until the wedding

Mother and daughter worked, side by side, in the kitchen of The Icing on the Cupcake. Piper Donovan mixed buttercream while her mother poured smooth batter into round baking pans. The front of the store was closed, the shelves emptied of the rolls, Danishes, and coffee cakes eagerly purchased by the morning's many customers. The ever-present aroma of sweet delights wafted throughout the building.

With her long blond hair pulled back in a ponytail, Piper stood at the table laden with bricks of butter, cartons of eggs, and bags of flour and sugar. She picked up a flower nail—a thin, two-inch-long metal rod with a small, round platform affixed to the end—and secured a square of parchment paper to it. Holding the flower nail in one hand, she applied firm and steady pressure to the plump bag she held with the other. Piper concentrated on the stream of stiff buttercream icing that oozed out from the piping tip and fashioned it into an acorn shape on top of the parchment. Then, picking up another decorating bag, with a different tip, she piped a wide strip as she turned the nail, cloaking the top of the acorn completely. Piper slowly spun the nail, making longer petals that overlapped again and again. When she reached the bottom, she had created a perfect yellow rose.

She repeated the process over and over, gently sliding the parchment squares with the finished roses onto baking sheets before storing them in the refrigerator.

"You've gotten so good at it, Piper," said her mother as she leaned forward to get a closer look at the flowers.

Piper shrugged and smiled mischievously. "And all those years you complained I never paid attention to you," she said.

"I really appreciate you taking the time to do this, honey," said Terri Donovan. "It's getting so I can't keep up with everything. I hated to do it, but I even had to turn down three wedding cake orders. Having these flowers made in advance will really help me at the end of the week when I have to make the cake I did promise to do."

"It's no big deal. I had to come out again anyway with more of my stuff. Might as well do these while I'm here." *But it is a big deal if my mother's turning down wedding cake orders,* she thought.

"Do you have much more to bring back?" asked Terri as she sifted confectioners' sugar into a mixing bowl.

"A few more cartons and the rug," said Piper, squeezing out a final delicate yellow flower. "I sold pretty much all the furniture and the kitchen things to the guy who is taking over my apartment."

"Good," said Terri. "None of it owes you anything. We found most of it at tag sales and, when the time comes for you to get another place, we'll be able to find more."

As she brought the decorating utensils to the sink and began washing them, Piper was thinking about getting back to the city and the audition she had in the morning.

Terri reached out and touched her daughter's arm. "It's going to be great having you back home, Piper," she said softly.

As Terri spoke, her eyes were trained over Piper's shoulder.

Piper turned around to see whom her mother was looking at. There was nobody else in the kitchen. "What are you looking at, Mom?"

"I'm looking at *you,* honey."

"Uh, no. No, you're not. You were looking at something behind me."

"I was not," insisted Terri. She nodded in the direction of the cleaned piping tips. "Make sure you put everything back exactly where you found it."

"Got it, Mom."

Strange. Was her mother losing it? Usually she was pretty laid-back, but recently she had become almost maniacal about having everything in its place. And there were other things Piper had noticed. On Thanksgiving, her mother missed a few of the glasses when she poured the apple cider. She had ruined the gravy, stirring in confectioners' sugar instead of flour. And when a customer handed Terri a $10 bill this morning, she pulled change for $20 from the register. Thank goodness they had honest customers.

Piper hadn't really thought much about each individual event, but now, as she concentrated on the decorating, she realized something was up. "Mom, is something wrong?" she asked gently.

Piper observed that her mother's jaw tightened as she shook her head.

"No, nothing's wrong, Piper. Just too much to do and not enough time to do it. I guess I'm a little tense, and when you're tense, you make mistakes."

Piper didn't buy it, but she kept silent. She knew she was on the brink of having to set major boundaries with her parents about her own privacy. So it was only fair that she gave her mother hers.

As she carefully arranged the piping tips in their container, Piper knew that, soon enough, she would figure out what was going on with her mother. When you lived in the same house with someone, there was no place to hide.

Unfortunately, that worked both ways.

Chapter 2

Monday, November 29 . . .
Twenty-five days until the wedding

Some people were named for beloved relatives, honored historical figures, favorite characters in fiction, or admired movie stars. Piper was named after her mother's passion: Terri Donovan was never happier than when she was piping sweet icing on a wedding cake.

Pacing back and forth in the hallway of the rehearsal studio on Manhattan's West Side, Piper found her mind wandering. Based on her mother's criteria, if Piper were to have a daughter, what would she name her? *Encore? Brava? Ovation?*

The door to the audition room opened, and a young woman emerged. She looked very similar to Piper and the other four girls waiting in the hallway. Piper braced herself, knowing she was next on the list. Her heart pounded.

"Piper Donovan?"

Breathe, she told herself, wondering how she had survived all twenty-seven years of her life, even though everyone thought she didn't breathe well enough. Her acting teachers, her karate, yoga, and Pilates instructors, her mother and father were always reminding her: "Just take a deep breath, Piper."

Entering the audition room, Piper studied the man sitting behind the long table. The casting director would size her up within just a few seconds and determine if she was right for the role. His laptop computer was open as he finished tapping in his notations about the previous actress.

The man turned his attention to the pile of photographs on the table and picked up Piper's head shot. "Good morning, Piper. I see here you spent a couple of seasons on *A Little Rain Must Fall*," he said as he scanned the information printed on the back.

Piper nodded. "Until they killed me—uh, I mean, until they killed off my character."

"Tell me about your character."

"I played Maggie Lane's long-lost younger sister, Mariah, who was always wreaking havoc. Neither of our characters was aware that we weren't actually related, but, you know how the soaps are, the viewing audience knew that we weren't really sisters. Glenna

Brooks, who plays Maggie, is, like, über-tiny, brown-eyed, and dark-haired. I'm obviously tall, with the whole 'green-eyes-and-blond-hair' thing. They had me dye it platinum for the role. I was into it, so I kept it that way."

"How did you die?"

"DWI. The writers wanted a cautionary tale."

"Big deathbed scene?"

"Yeah—eleven days! It's a soap; you die in installments."

The director smiled. "And I see you did a shampoo commercial," he said, glancing at the head shot again. "*That's* where I know you from! You're the girl on the horse with the mane of golden hair. That commercial used to be on during the first season of *Glee*."

Piper nodded. "I wish it was still running in prime time. Miss the residuals."

The director returned to the information on the back of the photograph. "So what have you been doing lately?"

Um, giving myself pep talks, thought Piper, but she answered with the standard "Oh, you know. Reading a lot of new scripts."

"How are you paying the rent?"

Piper shrugged. "I waitress."

"Where?"

"The Sidecar above P. J. Clarke's."

"Which P. J. Clarke's?"

"The original one at Fifty-fifth and Third."

"There's a restaurant above there?"

"Yeah, it has a separate entrance with a doorbell and a more sophisticated menu, but they still have the burgers."

"Huh. I'll have to check it out."

"You should."

She wondered how this happened so often. How did she end up spending more time on the merits of P. J. Clarke's than on her actual audition? *Mind-blowing.*

As if he were reading her mind, the director asked, "What do you like about this role?"

Piper hesitated. The fact was, there wasn't much she liked about the role. It was too close. She was coming off her own epic romantic failure, and playing a woman with a broken heart night after night would really just be masochistic. But Gabe, her agent, insisted she was perfect for it. Gabe, love bug that he was, thought she was right for every role. Bummer that Gabe wasn't a casting director.

When the audition was over, Piper couldn't even remember what words she had strung together in response to the question. She hoped they were coherent. All she knew was that before she got halfway through her monologue, the casting director turned his attention away from her and back to his laptop. When she was done, he thanked her but made no further comments. Piper knew she wasn't going to get the part.

Still, as she gathered up her coat and scarf in the hallway outside the audition room, she allowed herself to hope that maybe she was wrong. For Piper, hope was everything.

As she made her way toward the exit, Piper pulled out her BlackBerry and switched the ringtone from silent to normal.

"Ohmigod! It's Mariah Lane!" The squeal came from a pair of young women exiting the Starbucks a few yards away.

"It totally is!" cried one of them in a stage whisper. "She was the best part of *A Little Rain Must Fall.*"

Both women made a beeline to the target of their enthusiasm.

"Hi, I'm Piper Donovan." She held out her hand.

"Oh, we know who you are. We love you!" said one of them, giggling. "We hated when they got rid of you."

"We follow you on Twitter and we're friends on Facebook," said the other.

"Good one! I'm actually just about to send out a tweet," said Piper. "Why shouldn't it be about the two of you? What are your names?"

"Oh, awesome. I'm Heather and this is Nina."

Piper tapped out the letters with her thumbs:

JUST MET NINA AND HEATHER WHO SAY THEY LOVE ME.
LOVE THEM!

The girls didn't have any paper, so they insisted Piper sign their Starbucks cups. As Piper used the blue highlighter that she kept in her bag for marking scripts, to scribble her autograph on the still-warm cups, she had to laugh. Was it pathetic that this was totally making her day?

Still, Piper felt grateful that she had been given a sign. She wasn't forgotten and she was on the right path.

Her luck was going to change.

Chapter 3

There was a giant window on each side of the entry to The Icing on the Cupcake. One offered a view of tempting layer cakes, brownies, cookies, and pastries displayed on colorful hand-painted plates resting on glass shelves and pedestals. The other allowed people on the sidewalk to watch Terri Donovan decorate her beautiful cakes.

Nothing gave Terri more pleasure than seeing the delight on the faces of family, friends, and customers as they admired her creations. She was expert in squeezing out buttercream stars, shells, flowers, hearts, vines, dots, and bows in every conceivable configuration. Equally important, she had a wonderful eye for color. The combination of her skill and imagination added up to culinary works of art.

The Icing on the Cupcake was Terri's dream come true. When her children were very young, years before she actually had her own bakery, Terri had dreamed of what she wanted her place to be. It wouldn't be large, and the variety of baked goods might be limited, but everything for sale would be luscious and almost sinfully pleasurable—the types of desserts that made people take a bite, close their eyes, and groan with pleasure.

Terri was determined that presentation would count at her establishment. Her cakes weren't going to be sold on circles of cardboard. They would be purchased and served at home on a pretty piece of flowered porcelain or painted pottery. The plate would be Terri's gift to her customer. Season after season, Terri purchased odd pieces and partial sets of china at tag sales and thrift shops, storing them in the basement of her split-level home, to the point where she could barely make her way to the washing machine, and her husband couldn't get to his tool bench and the rest of his "man cave."

Now, The Icing on the Cupcake was in its fifteenth year, and the stacks of plates in the Donovans' basement had long since been depleted. But Terri and her friend Cathy still trawled the garage sales to replenish their stock. Customers, too, came in carrying plates they had received with past purchases, recycling them, and always buying another cake on another plate before they left.

The idea to decorate her cakes in the window for all the world to see came to Terri when she, Vin, and the kids took a rare vacation to visit relatives in Sarasota, Florida. The sidewalk in front of a local fudge shop was always crowded with people craning their necks to watch as the molten mixtures of chocolate, sugar, milk, and butter were poured from shiny copper pots onto huge white marble slabs. The fudge maker, clad in an immaculate uniform, folded and spread the mixture back and forth, back and forth, as it gradually cooled and was shaped into long bars of candy. Viewers were mesmerized, and Terri noticed most of them ended up going into the shop to buy. Terri added the picture window to her plan.

When Piper and Robert were both in school full-time, Terri got a job at the Hillwood Bakery. She worked the counter for eight years while perfecting her skills. When the owner decided he wanted to retire, Terri and Vin Donovan took out a loan, purchased the business, and Terri got her chance to implement her long list of ideas.

Now Terri, her curly hair covered with a net, squinted as she worked at her table. The sun streaming through the window caused a bothersome glare, to which she found herself becoming more and more sensitive over the last months. She picked up her pair of light-yellow-tinted glasses, positioned them over her prescription ones, and tried to concentrate.

She was terrified that all she had worked for could be coming to an end.

Chapter 4

A disheveled man wearing a torn jacket, filthy pants, and woolen gloves with the fingertips cut off sat huddled over a heating grate in the sidewalk.

Piper took a $5 bill from her wallet and handed it to him. "Merry Christmas," she said. "Food. Promise me you'll use it for food."

The man didn't say a word but gave Piper a wide grin revealing several missing teeth.

The biting winter wind pounded against Piper's body as she kept her head down and continued trudging up Ninth Avenue. Christmas wreaths and colored lights draped storefronts and restaurant windows. The sidewalk was crowded with workers and shoppers rushing to buy presents or meet friends and business associates for holiday luncheons. Piper was thrilled to be part of the latter group. She always loved spending time with Glenna.

Piper knew that by the end of their lunch, memories of the lackluster audition would be replaced by whatever Glenna had to say. Rejection was a regular part of any actor's life, and Piper had become quite adept at moving on. The disappointments still hurt, and there were days when tears were inevitable, but after years of never understanding what she had done wrong, Piper had found ways to prevent the sting of it from intruding on her social life.

To Piper, this was it. There was simply nothing that made her happier than acting or rehearsing or watching other actors. She had gotten a college degree because her parents had insisted, but Piper had wished away those four years. All she had ever wanted to do was act . . . and fall in love.

That goal was eluding her so far. After six months, she was still explaining to some people that she wasn't getting married after all. The broken engagement, not of her doing, had left her reeling but philosophical. Better to be done with the relationship before proceeding to a wedding ceremony and a couple of kids.

Secretly, Piper worried that this was becoming a most unfortunate pattern. During high school and college, she had lived for each new episode of *Sex and the*

City and eagerly awaited her time to pursue love in Carrie Bradshaw's magical metropolis. Now, Piper had plenty of material for a season's worth of episodes.

Before her ex-fiancé, Gordon, there was Bill, the guy she'd gone out with for over a year only to find out that he was engaged to somebody else; and Jeffrey, the one who watched and commented on everything she ate, reminding her in no uncertain terms that, if they were to marry, weight gain would be grounds for divorce; and Tom, the one who was happiest when his mother accompanied them to dinner. Piper had tried to ignore it for a few months, but when she caught Tom taking his mother's hand one night while the three of them sat together in a movie theater, she knew she had to end it.

Despite all the false starts, Piper believed in love, in following dreams, and in happy endings. But with her acting career stalled and her bank account running on empty, she needed some time to take a step away and, hopefully, breathe. She wondered what Glenna would say when she told her that she was giving up her apartment at the end of the month, eliminating the rent-check panic, and moving back to her parents' house in the New Jersey suburbs.

Going home to live with Mommy and Daddy for a while.

She was pretty sure Carrie Bradshaw had never done that.

While she waited at the restaurant, Piper ordered a glass of the cheapest merlot on the menu, picked out a piece of Italian bread from the basket on the table, and took out her BlackBerry. She had several messages on her voice mail. The first was from Glenna Brooks.

"I'm going to be a little late, Piper, but I have a *big* surprise. Big and great. Can't wait to tell you. See you soon."

Piper guessed that Glenna had gotten the part in that film she wanted or that the soap's writers were creating an even more outrageous story line for her. Viewers loved the Maggie Lane character. They were excessively blogging about everything, from what she was wearing to whom she was dating. Glenna received more fan mail than any actor on the show. It was common on the soaps to replace an actor for the same character when necessary, but for the *Little Rain* audience, Glenna Brooks *was* Maggie Lane. Glenna's agent had deftly used that popularity when negotiating her last contract.

Piper resolved that, whatever Glenna's news was, she was going to be stoked for her friend even though there was a lull in her own acting career.

Everyone has highs and lows. I'm just in a little down period. Eventually, things are going to get better.

Piper knew that Glenna had had her own down times, particularly in her personal life. She had gone through a miserable divorce while she and Piper worked together. That's when they had become friends.

Even though Piper was brand-new to the show, she and Glenna had connected immediately. Piper was younger and far more green than Glenna, but the star treated Piper as an equal. She ended up confiding in Piper about the challenges of divorce, especially when the gossip columnists were paying attention. Despite Piper's insistence that she'd feel different eventually, Glenna vowed that she would never marry again.

These conversations had helped them bond. Glenna became a Piper Donovan champion, sharing theatrical contacts and praising her acting talent to various people in the industry.

Since Piper left the show, they hadn't seen each other as much. In fact, Piper realized that they hadn't really talked in several months. They'd scheduled this holiday lunch to catch up. Piper was especially curious about the recent announcement that *A Little Rain Must Fall,* in an effort to cut production costs, was leaving New York and following so many of the other soaps out to Los Angeles.

The waiter placed the glass of wine on the table. Piper took a sip as she listened to the next message.

"Piper, it's me. Thanks again for doing those roses for me yesterday, honey. We can't wait for you to get out here. Daddy is almost finished painting your room. I think you're going to like it, sweetheart. Got to go, the brownies need to be iced. Call me when you can. Love, Mom."

Piper smiled to herself. Her mother always signed off on voice messages as if she were dictating the close to a letter. Once, when she had been really annoyed at Piper, she closed a terse voice-mail message with "Sincerely, Mom." But Piper's brow knit in concern as she thought about the "painting your room" thing. It made her nervous. Painting her old room indicated that they wanted to make her feel excited about coming home—and that they expected her to stay a long time. While Piper had repeatedly told them this was a short-term move, her parents had never been crazy about their only daughter residing in Manhattan. Since Piper had been jilted, they had been truly worried about her living alone in the Big City at such a vulnerable time in her life.

She knew that her parents just wanted to take care of her. While Piper loved them for that, she didn't need to be smothered. Piper had made them promise that they would chill out a bit and treat her like an adult. As long as they didn't ask her too many personal questions and didn't start tracking her comings and goings, this could work out.

But she knew her parents. It would be next to impossible for them to keep those promises.

I'm crazy to be doing this, aren't I? Of course I am. But the die has been cast. I've given up my lease. It won't be for long, it won't be for long. It's a vacation, really. A chance to relax and regroup. That's all it is. It can't be for long.

Piper swiped the bread in the little dish of olive oil and popped it in her mouth as she listened to the next message.

"Hi, Pipe, it's Jack. Hope the audition went well. Don't forget, dinner at my place tonight. I still refuse to believe it's your farewell. See you about seven."

Piper had been trying not to dwell on all of the aspects of Manhattan life she would miss, but the thought of not having regular dinners with Jack Lombardi made her ache. They had become close friends and confidantes in the two years since they met at a karate class. Over many pasta dinners and countless bottles of wine, Jack had listened to Piper's ramblings about life as an actor and her intense desire to find true and lasting love. Jack thought every guy who had treated

Piper badly was a total loser and he had offered, more than once, to teach them a lesson. Piper was never quite sure if Jack actually meant it or not. He didn't say much about his work with the FBI, but when he sheepishly shared details of the way he himself had sometimes treated some of the women *he* dated, Piper was glad that her relationship with Jack was a platonic one. She repeatedly told herself that Jack Lombardi was a friend, not a lover.

The last message was from her agent, Gabe Leonard.

"Listen, baby, I can get you in at the last minute to audition this afternoon for a cat food commercial. It's local. The cat is the star and there are no lines for you, but I wanted to let you know about it. Call me if I should let them know you're coming. Call me anyway. I want to hear how the audition went this morning."

You've got to be kidding me. Piper always felt extremely guilty on the rare occasions she turned down an audition. But, really, she'd been having a particularly rough couple of weeks, so the thought of rushing through a lunch that she'd been so looking forward to, to fawn over some lame brand of cat food, made her want to regurgitate her bread.

She was allergic to cats, too.

Piper used the last reason when she texted her answer to Gabe. She'd call him later. She was in no rush to discuss the morning's audition. Piper was about to update her Facebook status when Glenna made her entrance.

While not much more than five feet tall, Glenna had the presence of a supermodel—and the world was her runway. Smiling brightly, her head held high, Glenna wore her gorgeous fur coat with confidence, ignoring political correctness. Some of the diners recognized her, some did not, but all of them watched her as she strode to the table. Piper was mesmerized too, at first, not even noticing the man following behind Glenna.

Piper stood up and the two women embraced in a flurry of "hello"s and "can you believe how long it's been"s. Then, Glenna reached out, took the man's arm, and steered him forward.

"Piper, I want you to meet Casey Walden."

She shook the man's warm, strong hand. "Nice to meet you," she said.

He was tall, fair-skinned, fair-haired, and wore a well-tailored camel-hair overcoat with a red cashmere scarf. As he put his arm around Glenna's shoulders, Piper immediately recognized the watch that peeked from beneath his shirt cuff. She had seen one like it on eBay when she had been trying to figure out a way to swing a used Cartier tank watch. The quest had proved fruitless. The timepiece was definitely not in her immediate future, but she had spent over an hour scrolling around to see what the options were. So she knew that the watch Casey Walden wore was worth well over $10,000. As the three stood, the waiter came over to them. "Should I set another place?" he asked.

"No," said Glenna. "That won't be necessary. Casey can only stay for a little while. Just bring another chair and a bottle of your best champagne, please."

Piper was relieved. She wasn't in the mood to make polite conversation with someone she didn't know. She had been planning to have a private chat with Glenna, and Casey would be an obstacle to that.

The waiter uncorked the bottle with an understated pop and poured a little of the sparkling liquid into Casey's glass. As he reached for the stem of the glass, Piper noticed that Casey's nails were bitten to the quick.

Glenna took hold of Casey's hand. "We have some wonderful news, Piper. I know it'll sound crazy, since you've never even met Casey before, but we're getting married on Christmas Eve. Get your dress and line up a date!"

"What? No! That's so exciting!" She reached over the table to pull Glenna close. "Congratulations," she whispered. "I'm so happy for both of you."

"It's all happened so fast, but Casey is the most incredible guy," said Glenna after her fiancé had said good-bye and left the restaurant. "I guess I can thank Susannah and her academic struggles for all this. Who knew the science teacher at her school would end up being so terrific? We met at a parent-teacher conference at the end of September, he proposed last weekend, and now, here we are getting married. It's been such a whirlwind, Piper."

"He's a teacher?" asked Piper. "Man, that school must pay really well. He seemed so, I don't know, well groomed, I guess."

Glenna laughed. "Inherited. His brother runs the family jewelry business."

"Wait! Not Walden's on Madison Avenue?" asked Piper, making the connection.

"That's the one," said Glenna. "Casey hasn't paid much attention to the business. But that's starting to change."

"And is that one of the 'family jewels'?" Piper asked, pointing to the large diamond on Glenna's left ring finger. "That's not a rock. It's a boulder! I'm surprised you can still lift your hand!"

"It's beautiful, isn't it? I'm so happy, Piper—the last two months have been like a dream."

"Well, you hear about it," said Piper, "but I never really knew anyone who met and decided to get married that quickly." She couldn't help but think to herself, *I hope you're doing the right thing.*

"I know," said Glenna. "How lucky am I?"

"And you said you'd never get married again."

"I lied." Glenna smirked.

"So how will you do the show?" asked Piper. "Are you going to commute or is Casey going to give up his job and move out to L.A. with you?"

"Neither," said Glenna.

"What do you mean?"

"I'm leaving the show."

"No!" exclaimed Piper. "Really?"

Glenna nodded. "I'm ready, Piper. I want to stay here in New York. I don't want to uproot Susannah, and flying back and forth between coasts all the time is no way to start a marriage. I want to get it right this time."

It was hard for Piper to imagine anyone giving up a starring role like Glenna's.

"How's everyone taking it?" asked Piper.

"Everyone's been great about it, except Quent, of course. He wasn't exactly thrilled." Glenna frowned. "I guess I understand. When I suggested that my leaving would shake things up and be a good thing for the show, he growled that he was worried enough about shooting with a new crew in L.A., and didn't need to be dealing with a new star as well."

"How 'bout Susannah? What does she think?"

"She's conflicted. She likes Casey well enough, but her loyalty is to her father."

"Are you inviting Phillip to the wedding?" Piper asked.

"I doubt it, unless Susannah insists," Glenna answered. "As far as I'm concerned, it would be absolutely fine if I never saw Phillip again. When I think about the crap I put up with from him . . ." Glenna let out a deep sigh. "Calling me at work twenty times a day to make sure I was there, drilling me with questions about who I was spending my time with. So suspicious and jealous. It's a wonder the marriage lasted as long as it did. I was a fool to hang on so long."

"Don't dwell on that, Glenna. This time will be different."

"I hope so." Glenna traced the rim of her wineglass and grew quiet.

"What's wrong?" asked Piper.

"It's probably nothing," said Glenna.

"What?"

"Well, maybe it's somebody's idea of a joke, but I received an anonymous letter in the mail. It said terrible things about Casey. It made it seem like I would be making a big mistake by marrying him."

"That's weird. Who would send something like that?" asked Piper.

Glenna shook her head. "I have no idea, but I have the letter with me. Want to see it?"

"Give it here," said Piper.

Glenna fished through her oversize Chanel bag, pulled the letter out, and handed it across the table.

Piper examined the letter and its envelope.

It was unsigned. And the text was printed in capital letters.

*NOT ALL LOVERS ARE TRIED AND TRUE
AND THE ONE YOU'VE FOUND
IS WORSE THAN MOST. A CLUE:
WHAT GOES AROUND COMES AROUND.
SO WATCH YOURSELF—HE'S SUCH A RAT.
STAY CLEAR WHEN IT'S CASEY AT THE BAT.*

"Why would someone send something like that, Piper?"

"Beats me." Piper shrugged. "Do you want me to show it to my FBI friend?" she offered. "I don't know what he'll say, but it's worth a shot."

"Would you?" asked Glenna, looking relieved. "That would be great, Piper. I don't really want to go to the police with it. That would end up being such a hassle."

"Sure," said Piper. "I'm having dinner with Jack tonight."

"Thanks. I so appreciate it," said Glenna. "And on a happier note, I have another favor to ask."

"Shoot."

"Remember how you used to bring in those cupcakes from your mother's bakery to the set?"

Piper nodded.

"I loved those things. Everybody did. They were so beautifully decorated and absolutely delicious."

"Uh-huh."

"Well, I was wondering if your mother would make my wedding cake. It's my second marriage and we're definitely keeping it low-key. It will be a relatively small and intimate reception and having the wedding cake come from your family's bakery would mean a lot to me."

"Of course she will. Anything for the bride," said Piper as the waiter arrived with their food. Her mother's remark about turning down wedding cake orders crossed Piper's mind, but she was confident her mother wouldn't say no to Glenna. "But what about your party planner? Won't she want to take care of the cake?"

"I've already told her I have a sentimental reason for having the cake made by your mother's bakery," said Glenna. "She didn't fight me on it."

———

"Let me," said Glenna, reaching for the check at the end of the meal.

"I should be treating you to celebrate your happy news," protested Piper.

"Knowing your mother will do the cake is a big enough treat," said Glenna, taking her credit card out of her wallet. "But you know what else you could do for me?"

"Name it."

"There's a charity auction next Thursday at Susannah's school. I'm on the organizing committee and Casey is the faculty adviser. Why don't you come and see the space where we'll be having our reception? And some of the *Little Rain* cast and crew will be there, too. It'll be good for them to see your face again. You never know . . ."

Chapter 5

The taxi drove through Central Park. Casey Walden sat in the backseat, looking out the window at the leafless trees. His brow was furrowed and his mouth was set in a deep frown.

How was he going to be able to hold his own financially in his relationship with Glenna?

Their romance had been a wonderful, unexpected gift. The past few months had brought him more pleasure than he had ever thought possible. He loved Glenna, loved everything about her.

She was nothing at all like the image he'd had about beautiful-but-difficult actresses. As they spent a fabulous autumn together, Casey had learned that Glenna preferred a picnic in the park in jeans over a formal dinner—though they had gone to several of those, charity events where Glenna lent her name and donated her time to make sure the evenings were successful.

He knew that Glenna was self-made, having been brought up in a family where money was tight. She had moved to New York all alone and put herself through acting school. There had been some very lean years, living with three other young women in a one-bedroom apartment, subsisting on whatever was on sale in the grocery store, scraping together enough to continue her acting classes.

To look at Glenna now, no one would think she had ever had a bad day. But she had. Bad days and bad years. Even as her career blossomed, she was in a horrible marriage.

Casey had met Phillip Brooks. He was a large man with broad shoulders and big, powerful hands. The rage in his dark eyes was palpable.

When Casey pressed Glenna for information on why the marriage had ended, she didn't offer details. She said Phillip's jealousy and possessiveness bothered her as much as his dishonesty. She had wanted to divorce Phillip in the years before he was sent to prison, but didn't, out of concern for Susannah and fear of how Phillip would react.

When Phillip was incarcerated, Glenna realized how peaceful the apartment was without him and how truly destructive it had been living with tension and being barraged with anger all the time. She came to the conclusion that Susannah would really be better off growing up in a tranquil home. Glenna also knew she herself didn't want to go back to the old situation when Phillip was released. She instituted divorce proceedings.

Glenna had confided that she thought she would never marry again. She had her daughter, she had her career, and she had more money than she had ever imagined having. She didn't want to rock the boat. But somehow—miraculously, as far as Casey was concerned—Glenna had fallen deeply in love with him and was willing to take the chance.

But now that they were actually going to be married, Casey was feeling uncomfortable.

He brought his finger to his mouth and gnawed at the nail. He didn't want Glenna to ever regret her decision. He wanted to take care of her and he didn't want to feel like a kept man. Intellectually, Casey knew it shouldn't matter which spouse brought in more money. Husband and wife were a team. But the idea of contributing his pathetically small private-school salary while Glenna supplied the big bucks grated on him.

There was a solution. There was a way for Casey to have a greater income. It was perfectly legal and his right to take more money from the family business.

But his brother was standing in the way.

Chapter 6

Terri divided the fluffy contents of a large bowl into three smaller ones. She added red concentrated icing gel to one of the containers. But as she mixed the dye into the white frosting, the resulting pink shade appeared much lighter than she knew it should have. Terri's first urge was to add more red, but she held back.

"Cathy," she called. "When you get a minute, come over here, will you?"

Terri waited while her dear friend and assistant finished ringing up a customer's order and then came over to the window.

"My feet are killing me." Cathy winced. "What's up?"

"I want your opinion. What do you think of this pink?"

"For what?"

"Roses for the Cunningham baby's christening."

"I thought they had a boy."

"No, a girl this time."

Cathy peered into the bowl of icing. "Perfect," she said.

"Not too pale?" asked Terri.

"Uh-uh." Cathy looked at Terri. "You know, I don't get it. You've been asking me a lot lately what I think of your colors. You've been coming up with just the right shades for years and you sure don't need my advice. What's going on?"

Before Terri could answer, customers came into the bakery. While Cathy waited on them, Terri got the time she needed to collect her thoughts. It had gotten to the point where she wasn't going to be able to hide it anymore.

Normally, she and Cathy shared pretty much everything of any importance. Terri had been feeling uncomfortable because she'd been holding back on something so major in her life, but she just hadn't wanted to talk about it. She had needed to get used to the idea first.

Terri had kept the secret during all the stages she'd worked through. First, she had denied that she even had a problem, and she waited for it to pass. After she knew for certain it wasn't going to go away, the fear set in—and then the anger.

Why is this happening to me?

Finally, Terri had come to accept it and knew that if she wanted her beloved business to survive, she was going to have to make some changes. She had a game plan and Cathy was going to have to play a very important role in carrying it out. The time had come to share what was happening.

When the customers had gone, Terri walked behind the counter, pulled Cathy to the side, and began to speak in a low voice.

"My pinpoint vision is failing. So is my depth perception, not to mention that colors are fading for me."

Cathy listened, slack-jawed, as Terri explained.

"It's macular degeneration."

"You're going blind?" Cathy blurted out.

"No, at least I sure hope not. It's very rare that it will cause total blindness. But it really affects quality of life, because it causes blurring right in the middle of my vision. It's like there's this blockage in the center of everything I look at. I can see around the edges though."

"How long has this been happening?"

"Actually, it hit one eye over a year ago, but the good eye let me function pretty much normally. Now, it's in both eyes."

"But I don't understand," said Cathy. "You've been doing everything you've always done, baking, mixing icing, decorating. How can you do that if you can't see well?"

Terri shrugged. "As far as the baking goes, I know that part pretty much by heart. I don't have to be able to see to know how much flour or how many eggs go into a cake. I've adapted some things I do, like dipping into the flour and sugar with my measuring cup instead of pouring from the bag, because I can't judge the distance and I miss most of the time. And I don't know if you've noticed, but there are raised marks now on the oven dials that let me know what temperature I'm setting."

"I did," said Cathy, "but I thought it was just a convenience thing so you wouldn't have to pay attention when you sct it."

Terri looked down at the bowl of pink icing. "But it's the decorating that's really giving me problems. Colors have become much less bright and intense. In fact, that's one of the first things I noticed. I found myself putting more and more coloring in the frosting to bring it up to the shade I wanted. It wasn't until longtime customers commented that I was taking a new, more vibrant direction in my color schemes, when I thought things looked the same as usual, that I realized something was really wrong. And, as for the decorating, I've been trying to compensate by tilting my head so I can see with my peripheral vision. But that's not cutting it anymore. It's getting harder and harder to make the flowers and borders and anything else that requires detail work. It's getting impossible to do my job."

The enormity of what Terri was telling her washed over Cathy. Decorating cakes wasn't just Terri's profession, it was her passion. Tears welled up in Cathy's eyes.

"Oh, Terri, I'm so sorry," she said, her voice breaking.

"Hey, none of that," said Terri. "I need you to help me, not feel sorry for me."

"How did Vin take it when you told him?" asked Cathy, as she wiped at the corner of her eye.

"Not well, at first. You know him, such a worrywart. He's always afraid the sky is falling."

"Well, it is this time," said Cathy.

"Only if I let it."

"And Piper? Have you told her?" asked Cathy.

"No. She's had enough on her plate and I don't want her to feel trapped."

"What do you mean?" asked Cathy.

"It's enough of a trauma for Piper that she's moving home. I don't want her feeling that she has to adapt her life to help me," said Terri. "I'm going to keep it from her as long as I can. But I'm afraid she is starting to suspect something. You know Piper: she notices everything."

Chapter 7

"Y ou want to see if the spaghetti's done?"

Piper snared a single strand from the boiling water and dangled it carefully into her mouth. "It needs another minute or two," she said. "We want it al dente, but this is still hard in the center."

Jack concentrated on the frying pan in front of him, moving the bits of pancetta around, making sure that each tiny cube of pork got browned. "It's not too late, you know," he said. "You don't have to leave."

"Yes, I do," said Piper, as she began breaking eggs into a small bowl, whisking them into a nice froth. "Giving up my apartment is really the least of it. I can find another place—"

"Or move in with a friend for a while," Jack interrupted. "I've told you before, that couch in the living room opens up. I'd even sleep on it and you could have my bed."

Piper set the the bowl of beaten eggs on the counter and took two wineglasses out of the cupboard above the sink. She walked over to the bistro table just outside the kitchen, arranging the glasses at their places as she considered Jack's offer. For several reasons, she doubted the arrangement would work for very long.

"No, it's done," she said, raising her voice so Jack could hear her from the kitchen. "My parents are practically foaming at the mouth, they're so excited about it. I'd ruin their Christmas if I didn't come home."

"Who says you can't still be with them for Christmas?" Jack called back. "Not good enough, Pipe."

Pouring some Pinot Grigio into their glasses, Piper took a swallow and nodded. "I know. You're right. It's sad. It's like *Little Women*. I'm going back to Orchard House after the city's had its way with me. Except there's no dying sister waiting. It's the coward's way out."

"Wow. That's exactly how I would have described it."

She could hear the smirk in Jack's voice.

Piper returned to the kitchen, grabbed the pot holders, and lifted the heavy pot of pasta, being careful to keep her face away from the scalding steam as she emptied the spaghetti and boiling water into the colander she'd settled into the sink.

"I'm not the first one to go home for a while, Jack."

"Yeah, but you're the last one I'd have expected to do it."

"Me, too. But what can I say? It just is what it is right now. Let's drop it, all right?"

"Fine," Jack said coolly.

The two of them had made spaghetti alla carbonara so often, their movements were like a carefully choreographed ballet. Jack stood at the stove and Piper brought the colander over, dumping its contents into the frying pan. As Jack mixed the pancetta and pasta together, Piper poured the beaten eggs into the mound of spaghetti. They both watched the eggs turn into a smooth cream, warmed by the hot pasta. Jack continued to mix as Piper grabbed the mill and cracked black pepper into the mixture. Finally, she poured a small bowl of freshly grated Parmigiano Reggiano over the top.

After transferring the pasta into a large serving bowl, Jack carried their dinner to the table and, for a few minutes, they sat silently enjoying their meal.

Piper was savoring the moment and appreciating the effort Jack had put into making her farewell dinner a special one. She loved the idea of Jack Lombardi, tough-guy FBI agent, stopping at the Korean grocer to buy flowers, lighting the candles, and selecting the music that now played, rhythmic and sensual.

Piper broke the silence. "I love the 'rents, Jack, but they can be really out of control sometimes: Mom is the queen of unsolicited advice, and Dad with his emergency preparedness craziness. He can't relax and he's always 'getting ready' for a disaster."

"You can't blame him. He's seen a lot."

"I get that, but it's a bit much. I don't know how my mother stands it."

"Maybe she loves him?"

"Wow, and people wonder how you got into the Bureau," Piper teased. "But, seriously, something's up with her. I don't know what it is, but something's wrong."

"Why do you say that?"

"Several things I noticed, but especially the fact that the last few times I asked her about what she's doing special for the holidays at the bakery this year, she changed the subject. That's so not my mother. The woman thinks up her Christmas cakes and is practicing her designs by the Fourth of July. She lives for it. And she told me that she turned down three wedding cake orders because things have been too busy at the shop."

Jack shrugged and took a large swallow of wine. "Makes sense to me. It's smart not to overextend yourself."

"For someone else, maybe. But for my mother to turn down a wedding cake job is like you turning down a chance to go to a Yankees–Red Sox game. Decorating wedding cakes is her crack. It's like Obama and his BlackBerry: she needs it."

Piper started to stand, reaching for the empty plates.

"Uh-uh," said Jack. "You just sit there tonight."

Piper watched as Jack cleared the dishes away. The sleeves of his V-neck sweater were pushed up, revealing his muscular forearms. As he turned and carried the plates to the sink, she couldn't help but admire his tall, trim build and broad shoulders.

"Speaking of wedding cakes, want to go to a wedding with me?" asked Piper. "I had lunch with Glenna today and she's getting remarried on Christmas Eve."

"I hope it's to a guy who obeys the law this time," Jack answered from the kitchen.

"Actually, she's marrying one of the teachers at her daughter's school."

"Going the modest route, huh?"

"Not too modest," answered Piper. "The ring was amazing."

"Good for Glenna," said Jack, coming back and putting two espresso cups on the table. "You gotta give credit to someone who's willing to get back up on the horse."

Piper nodded, deep in thought.

"What?" asked Jack.

"I hope she's doing the right thing. Glenna's only known him for a few months and someone sent her a really bizarre note warning her not to marry him." Piper bit her lower lip.

"Oh no," Jack groaned. "Here it comes."

"What do you mean?"

"You told Glenna that you'd have me look at the letter."

"How did you know?"

"Because I know you and I can tell by the expression on your face that you volunteered me for something but you don't want to tell me because you think I won't like it." Jack rolled his eyes. "Hand it over," he said with resignation.

"Great," said Piper as she sprang up to get her purse. She pulled out the envelope and gave it to him.

Jack glanced at the white, business-size envelope. Glenna Brooks's address was printed on the front.

"I bet just about anyone could get her address if they really tried," said Piper. "You can find everything on the Internet if you look hard enough."

"Really, Sherlock? I didn't know that." Without commenting further, Jack took the letter from the envelope, unfolded it, and began to read. There was no salutation. Just a few lines of type on standard computer paper.

"'Stay clear when it's Casey at the bat,'" Jack repeated the last line. "I remember memorizing 'Casey at the Bat' when I was in fourth grade."

He handed the letter back to Piper. "This could be from anybody," he said, "but first I'd look at Glenna's ex-husband or find out if the groom-to-be has an old flame who doesn't want this wedding to go forward. But, if you want my opinion, I don't think whoever wrote this is really someone to worry about. My gut tells me this is just an amateurish, sour-grapes attempt to intimidate Glenna."

"That's it? Shouldn't you take it to a lab or something?"

"Come on, Pipe. Believe it or not, we've got a war on terrorism going on. You can't really expect me to have this dusted for prints or checked for DNA, can you?"

"No, I guess not," answered Piper, though that was exactly what she had been hoping he'd do.

Jack read the disappointment on Piper's face. "Look, if she wants to make it official and file a police report, she can. But there are lots of nut jobs out there who talk a good game but are harmless in the end. It's going to be hard to get the cops to devote any manpower or lab power to this based on that kooky letter. Want some sambuca with the espresso?"

Piper let the matter drop, knowing she wasn't going to get any further with Jack. They drank and laughed and drank some more. When Piper stood up to leave, she wobbled, grabbing hold of the edge of the table. Jack reached over to steady her. For a moment, he held her and pulled her close.

"I wish you'd stay," he said.

"Let's not get into that again. I'm leaving for my parents' in the morning and that's it."

"That's not what I meant," Jack whispered. "I wish you'd stay here tonight . . . with me." He reached out and put his arms around her, enveloping her in an embrace.

Piper closed her eyes, welcoming the warmth and strength of Jack's body. It would be easy to just let things progress. But Piper was scared. She and Jack had a good thing going, a tight friendship that she deeply valued. Bringing romance into it was taking a big risk. It would change things and, if it didn't work out, it could ruin what she really treasured.

"Whoa there, mister," Piper said as she forced herself to pull back. "Let's not do something we'll regret."

Chapter 8

Potassium cyanide seemed to make the most sense. It was available and could be mixed to contaminate common drinking water. Internet reports were conflicted about what the taste would be like, primarily because the people who could be trusted to know were dead.

The scent of almonds had been detected on the breath of some who had ingested cyanide, and there was a faint, bitter-almond odor to both cyanide gas and crystals. So there was speculation that there might be a bitter taste to a drink laced with it. But, if enough of it was used, by the time the drinker realized anything, it would be too late.

A lethal dose would require 200–300 milligrams. Taking into account that the crystals would be dissolved *in the water, and the victim probably wouldn't ingest the entire drink, it stood to reason that it would be best to mix in more. The Web helped with that too, suggesting the use of a scale, available for purchase for $5, to weigh out the necessary milligrams.*

Milligrams that devastated the central nervous system and heart. Milligrams that had led to the demise of Adolph Hitler, his bride, and his aides. Milligrams that were mixed with Kool-Aid at Jonestown and killed more than nine hundred men, women, and children. Milligrams swallowed by captured soldiers and spies to avoid the risk of divulging secrets under torture.

But all those milligrams had been ingested as suicides. The milligrams ingested at the Metropolitan School for Girls auction would be murder.

Chapter 9

Tuesday, November 30 . . .
Twenty-four days until the wedding

The Frenzied Barking began even before Piper inserted her key into the lock. As she opened the front door of her parents' home, the Jack Russell terrier sprang up to greet her.

"Hey, Emmett," Piper cooed, tossing down her bag on the floor of the small entry hall and bending down to embrace the dog. "How's my boy, huh?"

After several licks to Piper's cheek, the dog stood back on his hind legs, his front paws held out in anticipation.

"Sorry, Em," said Piper. "I don't have anything for you right now. I'll get you something to eat in a little bit."

The dog looked at her.

"Don't make me feel guilty, buddy," said Piper. "Please."

From the Saturday afternoon Piper and her mother had gone to the animal shelter and spotted the little white dog with the floppy ears and a big brown patch around his left eye, they were goners. Piper had still been working on *A Little Rain Must Fall,* and it was the week before she attended her first—and last—Daytime Emmy Awards ceremony. She'd named the terrier Emmett in honor of the occasion, only later realizing how appropriate the moniker would be. The dog could just as easily have been named for world-famous clown Emmett Kelly.

Happy-go-lucky and friendly, Emmett was very smart and responded exceptionally well to the obedience training Piper's father had insisted upon. But it was Piper's mother who cultivated the terrier's special talents, teaching him a series of tricks using food as a reward.

The dog had already provided the Donovan family and their neighbors with hours and hours of delight and laughter when Terri came up with the idea of having Emmett featured in commercials for the bakery, which ran on the local-access cable channel. As a result, Emmett had become something of a celebrity in Hillwood.

Piper gave Emmett another pat as she called out, "Anybody home?" While she brushed the dog hair from the sleeves of her coat, Piper heard her father's voice.

"Down here."

Piper went through the door at the end of the foyer and down the cement steps to the basement, where her father had created what they all called his "man cave." The walls were lined with wire-mesh shelving loaded with clearly marked, transparent plastic boxes filled with paraphernalia collected over many years. First-aid supplies from simple to borderline-combat-medic gear, signal mirrors, compasses, key rings, lanyards, water purifiers, Swiss Army knives, pocket-size wrenches and pry bars, folding screwdrivers, wind- and waterproof matches, duct and electrical tape, and long lengths of cord in widths ranging from dental floss to thick climbing rope.

Numerous books on first aid, survival, and travel sat on a shelf positioned next to a gun safe stocked with a .22 caliber rifle, a stainless-steel Ruger 10/22, a pump-action shotgun, a cowboy-type carbine, a .357 Magnum, and a companion Smith & Wesson .357 revolver. The weapons were not displayed, and Vin was fastidious about keeping the big metal cabinet locked. Only he had the combination needed to open it.

Vin said he hoped to never use any of the guns, but he was ready if necessary. He believed that the

Second Amendment of the Constitution meant what it said. He had a right to defend himself and his family.

Her father sat at a large utility table lit by a swing-arm lamp with a built-in magnifying glass. Vin looked up from the project he was working on and smiled at Piper.

"Good to have you home, lovey," he said.

"Thanks," she answered, giving him a kiss on the cheek. "Mom at the bakery?"

"Yup."

"What's on the agenda this time, Dad?" asked Piper, leaning down and putting her arm around his shoulders.

"Putting fresh batteries in the emergency kits."

Vin Donovan regarded life as a series of challenges and possibilities for which he and his family needed to be prepared. What if the car broke down? What if there was an ice storm and the power went out? What if his daughter was stranded in the subway?

He couldn't understand why everyone didn't think that way. He knew that people rolled their eyes and poked fun at his hypervigilance, but he didn't give a damn. Those same people showed up at his door when the power went out and they needed candles and batteries.

Everyone seemed to attribute Vin's actions to his years as a cop, but the fact was Vin had made his first kit when he was five years old—filled with a few Band-Aids, iodine, gauze, rolled cotton, a pair of tweezers, and a kid's small, blunt-nosed scissors.

For as long as he could remember, Vin had felt the need to be ready for any emergency. Even before Homeland Security devised its color-coded security advisory system soon after 9/11, he had lived his whole life at "Threat Level Orange."

Chapter 10

Friday, December 3 . . .
Twenty-one days until the wedding

Piper and Terri worked efficiently at the back of the bakery, packing Linzer tortes, ginger snaps, and sugar cookies in the shapes of bells, stars, and snowflakes, into pink boxes and tying them with green twine.

"Please, Mom," said Piper. "Say you'll do it. Glenna's been a good friend to me."

"I just can't take it on, Piper. I'm sorry."

"But I already told her you would."

"I told you, we're just too busy at Christmastime to make a Christmas Eve wedding cake."

"Mom. Think about it. It's Glenna Brooks. It's her wedding cake! For all we know, *InStyle Weddings* or *People* magazine will be covering it. Come on, think about the caption: 'Terri Donovan of The Icing on the

Cupcake captured Brooks's desire for both warmth and elegance with her three-tiered wedding cake.' You'll be the talk of Curves."

"I said no, Piper, and that's it."

Piper was stunned. She had been home for a few days now, and she had been coming into The Icing on the Cupcake to help in the kitchen and at the counter. While the store was definitely busy, it didn't seem any different from the usual holiday rush.

Terri reached for another box but knocked it onto the floor. Piper reached over to pick it up, noting to herself that her mother had missed the cup when pouring coffee earlier. She couldn't figure out why her mother wasn't looking her straight in the eyes.

"Something's wrong, isn't it, Mom?" asked Piper.

"No. Nothing's wrong. I'm just a little tired, I guess."

"Are you sure?"

"Yes, I'm sure," said Terri. "You know, Piper, if you really want this wedding cake done for your friend, why don't you make it?"

"Hilarious, Mom."

"Why not? You know how to decorate. You've been doing it since you were a little girl. And you've watched and helped me so many times."

It was true. Piper did know how to make pretty much everything her mother did. When Piper was growing up, Terri used to bake cakes for all the neighborhood kids. Each child would count the days until it was their turn to place an order from the photographs in the Wilton cake decorating books. Then Mrs. Donovan would work her magic to create the flavorful cake that looked almost identical to the enchanting images in the pictures. *Honestly,* Piper thought, *they turned out even better.*

Piper had stood at her mother's elbow, helping to mix buttercream and meringue, working with fondant and chocolate, practicing making shells and petals and leaves from icing. Once she was old enough, Piper worked after school on Fridays and on the weekends and helped her mother in the bakery. By the time she went off to college, Piper was almost as good as her mother at decorating cakes.

Piper considered her mother's suggestion. Maybe it wasn't so crazy. She had always liked decorating the cakes. Maybe it would be good for her to have something to keep her mind occupied. In a way, it was therapeutic to decorate a cake. It didn't allow you to think of anything else. Not old boyfriends or a stalled career. Nothing but the cake.

Piper had to admit that sounded pretty good right now.

"Would you help me?" asked Piper.

"I don't think you'll need much help," said Terri as her fingers counted off cookies. "But, yes, I will."

"You'll help me come up with the design?"

"Um-hmm," Terri answered. "But you need the bride's input on that. I have a list of questions I always ask my brides. I'll give it to you and you can ask Glenna."

Piper thought. "Man, I'll have to start practicing soon."

"Fine," said Terri. "There's a sheet cake for the Pacheco Christmas party ready to be done on the counter over there. She wants angels and stars. Get to it."

Chapter 11

Thursday, December 9 . . .
Fifteen days until the wedding

The Metropolitan School for Girls was housed in a Fifth Avenue mansion once owned by a prominent New York family. Built at the turn of the twentieth century, it was a five-story Beaux Arts masterpiece with a white marble facade, intricate carvings, and Ionic columns that flanked the entrance. Across the street, the Metropolitan Museum of Art and Central Park offered world-class opportunities to learn and play. There were some scholarship students, but most of the girls who attended the school were from families who were quite well-off financially.

Entering the building, Piper gave her coat to an attendant, checked in at the desk, and made her way through the grand reception area. An oil painting of a rolling landscape hung over an elaborate fireplace that graced almost one entire wall. On the other side of the room, a sweeping marble staircase began an ascent, circling upward to the floors above. Carved moldings lined the ceiling, an exquisite crystal chandelier sparkled above, and a large Oriental carpet covered the floor. The expansive space was crowded with well-heeled guests, mingling and drinking.

"Piper! There you are."

Glenna Brooks swept toward her, wearing a form-fitting green cocktail dress and carrying a champagne flute. Her hair was piled on top of her head and she wore dangling emerald earrings. She embraced Piper, who suddenly felt utterly unexciting in the black sheath she'd gotten at Loehmann's.

"I'm so glad you're here," said Glenna.

"Thanks for inviting me," said Piper. "This place is ah-mazing!"

"I know," said Glenna. "Won't it be perfect for the wedding? Just the right amount of space for the people we are inviting. Not too big, not too small." Glenna looked hopefully at Piper. "Did you ask your mother about making the cake?"

"My mother says she really can't, Glenna."

"Oh, no," said Glenna, dragging out the short words, her face registering her disappointment.

"I'm sorry, Glenna. But my mother had another idea and, if you're into it, it could work."

"What?"

"I could make the cake. My mother would be there to help with the design and keep me in check."

"You, Piper?" Glenna asked. "You know how to make a wedding cake?"

"I actually do," said Piper. "I've helped my mother lots of times. Don't worry, Glenna. I wouldn't offer if I didn't think I could handle it."

Considering for just a moment, Glenna shrugged. "Okay, why not? I trust you. What do we have to lose?"

"Oh, yay!" Piper exclaimed. "I'm so excited. When you and Casey have a few minutes, I have some questions to ask you."

"All right," said Glenna. "Maybe we can do it after the auction."

Piper opened her purse, took out the white envelope, and handed it to Glenna.

"You showed it to Jack?"

"I did," answered Piper, "but, to tell the truth, he wasn't too concerned. He thinks somebody is just jealous. Maybe an old love doesn't want to see you and Casey happy."

"Like Phillip?" asked Glenna.

"Maybe. Or somebody else. What about Casey? You think one of his exes could have, you know, gone off her meds?"

"Oh, who knows?" asked Glenna. She cocked her head toward the front desk. "See that woman checking everyone in? Her name is Jessie Terhune. She and Casey were involved for a while. Casey told me she was much more serious than he was. But I can't imagine that she'd actually write a letter like this."

Glenna frowned as she looked down at the envelope. Then she lifted her head and straightened up, shifting her shoulders back. "This is ridiculous," she said. "I'm not going to give whoever wrote this piece of trash the satisfaction of getting upset." She handed Piper a program. "In the meantime, check this out and see if there's anything you want to bid on. And Quent Raynor is over there. Make sure you go over and talk with him. You never can tell what's going on in that mind of his."

Glenna departed to check on some last-minute details. As she passed the fireplace, she tossed the envelope into the flames.

Chapter 12

Piper perused the list of auction items. Dinners at Rao, Per Se, and Jean Georges; New York Giants season tickets; box seats for the opera at Lincoln Center; a consultation with a leading plastic surgeon who was throwing in a series of Botox injections; a session with renowned photographer Martha Killeen; a diamond bracelet from Walden's; and a behind-the-scenes tour of *A Little Rain Must Fall* hosted by Travis York, Glenna's costar. Piper noted that Travis had also agreed to act as auctioneer for the evening, with Glenna acting as his assistant.

Piper had gotten to know and like Travis during her stint on the soap opera. She had always suspected that the love scenes his character played with Glenna's were more than acting, on his part. She had observed the way his eyes followed Glenna, the way he listened to her every word and was delighted by everything Glenna did. So when Glenna had confided the information that she and Travis eventually did have a short fling right after she and Phillip separated, Piper was not surprised.

Piper wondered how Travis felt about his costar getting married.

Scanning the room and looking for Quent Raynor, the head writer and main director of *A Little Rain Must Fall,* Piper spotted Martha Killeen holding a camera and talking to the woman who used to go out with Casey. *What was her name again? Jessie something.*

With her short red hair, freckles, and small, upturned nose, Martha Killeen was as well known to people in the entertainment world as those she photographed. Over the years, Martha herself had been the subject of magazine and newspaper articles touting her creative genius, her ability to dream up fabulous ways for her subjects to be photographed. No setting was too exotic, no costume too fantastic, no situation too outlandish if Martha thought they would enhance the photo shoot and end up expressing the essence of her subject's personality.

But lately, the articles about Martha Killeen mentioned her remarkable talent only in passing. Instead, they focused on the severe financial problems with which she was struggling. The last story Piper read reported that Martha had negotiated some time from her creditors.

For as long as she could remember, Piper had fantasized about having her picture taken by the award-winning photographer. During high school, she must have thumbtacked to her wall over a dozen portraits taken by Killeen found in assorted magazines. Some girls liked the Backstreet Boys; Piper liked Meryl Streep in black-and-white. Being photographed by Martha Killeen was like being asked to step into a work of art.

Piper could only imagine what the bidding would be later for the photo session. She knew that this wasn't going to be her chance to step in front of Killeen's lens, but there was nothing wrong with fantasies.

The diamond bracelet rested on a black velvet pillow. Piper stared at it with no particular longing. Jewelry wasn't her thing.

"Beautiful, isn't it?"

Piper looked up at the middle-aged man who stood next to her.

"If you're into that," she answered.

The man raised his eyebrows. "And you're not?" he asked.

Piper shrugged dismissively. "I'd rather have a Prius."

"You could have two of them for what that bracelet's worth," said the man.

Piper smiled. "Think the bracelet will bring that kind of money tonight?"

"I'm counting on it. I'm Arthur Walden."

It took Piper a second to make the connection. "Oh, Walden's Jewelers."

"Right."

"I'm Piper Donovan." She held out her hand. "Sorry about the comment."

He shook her hand perfunctorily. "No problem. To each his own."

"I'm a friend of Glenna's," said Piper. "You're Casey's brother?"

"That's right."

Arthur Walden was an older, heavier version of his brother, also fair-skinned and blue-eyed, but Arthur's blond hair was combed over from one ear to the other in a vain attempt to camouflage his receding hairline.

"I have to admit, that was a gorgeous ring Casey gave Glenna," said Piper. "I'm guessing it came from Walden's."

"Of course," said Arthur.

"It must be nice going to work every day, surrounded by such extraordinary things."

"It's been the family business for three generations," said Arthur. "But Casey never really developed a passion for it. He's more interested in astronomy and the stars than in anything sparkling in our jewelry cases."

"Not for long, I heard," said Piper. "Glenna told me he's planning on getting more involved at Walden's."

Arthur's face showed no emotion, but his voice betrayed annoyance. "Now that he's going to be a family man, all of a sudden Casey is a lot more interested in what's happening in the business. You'll excuse me, won't you?" he said abruptly. "I have to go find my wife."

Chapter 13

The caterers were set up in a room at the back of the mansion, which was now the student cafeteria. Long tables were covered with sparkling glassware, trays of finger foods, and cases of wine. The waiters scurried in and out, depositing empty trays and exchanging them for full ones prepared by the kitchen staff.

Jessie Terhune walked into the room, her mouth set in a tight line. She observed the organized chaos, wanting every single aspect of the evening to go right. Certainly not out of any desire to see the event, organized by the lovebirds, do well; she would relish seeing Glenna Brooks and Casey Walden crestfallen and embarrassed. But Jessie's department, the drama department, stood to benefit from every dollar raised this evening. At least, that had been the theory of it when she and Casey had originally talked last summer about having the auction. Now, there was talk that the drama department was only going to get a small slice of the proceeds and the rest would go to scholarships. Fetching a pitcher of water for the auctioneer, Jessie reflected on how quickly life could change. Just a few months ago, she and Casey were spending long days on Main Beach in East Hampton, lying in the sun, eating lobster rolls, and walking along the ocean's edge. Three generations of Waldens had enjoyed their summers on the eastern shore of Long Island in a sprawling shingled "cottage" with a garden full of rambling roses and bushy hydrangeas. Jessie had anticipated that her first summer there would not be her last.

One afternoon, as they walked up the beach in August, Jessie told Casey that she had just gotten word that her budget was being severely cut. The school's endowment had fallen off sharply and the board of trustees was demanding that operating expenses be reduced. The drama department budget had been whittled down to almost nothing.

Casey had come to the rescue, suggesting the fundraising auction. He'd offered to organize it and declared that he would get his brother to donate something wonderful from Walden's. Their enthusiasm grew as they brainstormed together about what they could obtain from the accomplished and connected parents of the students. By Labor Day, they had a long list of items they thought it could be reasonable to obtain as auction prizes. When the summer ended and they went back to school, Jessie looked forward to spending any free time she had working on the auction with Casey.

Then came parents' night. *My knight in shining armor found a new damsel,* Jessie thought. A beautiful queen who was famous to television viewers and magazine readers around the country. When Glenna Brooks heard that the auction was to benefit the drama department, she volunteered to be involved. Or so she said. Jessie was convinced that the reason the actress wanted to help with the auction was to spend more time with Casey.

As Jessie saw it, Glenna Brooks was overrated as an actress. Audiences loved her, but Jessie didn't understand the allure. It was amazing that Glenna had risen to such heights with such mediocre talent.

Those who can, do; those who can't, teach. The old saying flashed through Jessie's mind. But she wouldn't allow herself to dwell on the idea that she had only turned to teaching when her own acting career hadn't panned out.

Grudgingly, Jessie had to give the devil her due. Glenna had gotten her soap-opera friends involved, and that was adding excitement and glamour to the event. It galled her, though, to watch Glenna waltzing around tonight, acting like she owned the place. It bothered Jessie even more to see the way her former lover followed Glenna around like an eager puppy.

Jessie was trying her best not to show that she cared. She wondered if she was really pulling it off. She wondered if Casey had any idea that her heart still ached. She hoped not. When he had broken it off with her, Jessie had said she understood and told him there were no hard feelings. She said they could still be good friends as well as professional colleagues. She had her pride. Maybe she couldn't compete with Glenna in the looks and charisma departments, but she could hold her head up high and be proud of her own talents and accomplishments. She'd be damned if anyone was going to look at her with pity.

Anyway, Jessie hadn't given up. Casey and Glenna hadn't walked down the aisle yet. There was still time.

Chapter 14

Piper caught sight of Quent Raynor. He was talking to Glenna and he didn't look happy. Nor did she.

It must be killing Quent that Glenna's leaving the show, thought Piper.

Quent was the mastermind behind *A Little Rain Must Fall.* A total control freak, who needed to be on top of everything, Quent had led *ALRMF* to countless daytime Emmys, including nine for himself for writing and directing, as well as three for Glenna. Quent's story lines had made Glenna a star. And now, just as all the soaps were in serious danger of cancellation, Glenna was deserting the show.

Quent Raynor couldn't be a happy man.

Piper considered going over to say hello to Quent and rescuing Glenna. As she started toward them, she watched in disbelief as Quent grabbed Glenna's arm, the unexpected gesture spilling Glenna's drink all over the front of her green dress.

Quent dug into his pocket for his handkerchief, but Glenna didn't wait. She turned and walked away.

As if he could feel Piper's eyes upon him, Quent glanced her way. Piper was surprised and a bit apprehensive when he waved for her to come over.

"Hi, Quent." Piper held out her hand.

"I can't believe what I just did."

Piper wasn't sure what to say. Reassuring Quent that accidents happened didn't seem appropriate. He had deliberately grabbed Glenna's arm. Piper decided not to take it on. "How have you been?" she managed.

"I was just thinking about you the other day, Piper."

"You were?"

Quent nodded. "Yeah. We'll be needing you on the show again. Next week, actually."

He took off his glasses and rubbed the bridge of his nose. The gesture gave him away. She remembered that whenever the director was angry or frustrated that things weren't going smoothly on the set or that the ratings were down, he'd take off his glasses and rub at his nose. All the cast and crew recognized the sign and braced themselves for the inevitable outburst to follow. His diatribes could be vicious.

Piper cocked her head to the side and a puzzled expression came over her face. "Really? Is Mariah Lane coming back from the dead?"

"The entire writing department has been working on a huge dream sequence for the last week of episodes we shoot in New York before we move out to the West Coast. We've just decided to include as many of our past characters as possible. It's just a few days' work, but hopefully you'll be available?"

"I'll *make* myself available!" answered Piper, her pulse racing. "I'd love to come back."

"Great," said Quent, replacing his glasses. "Gabe Leonard is your agent, right? Have him call the casting office to work out the details."

Piper was so happy that she didn't let it bother her when Quent downed the rest of the wine in his glass and said he had to go out for a cigarette. In fact, she was relieved. She didn't want to be around if Quent had one of his tantrums.

Chapter 15

*T*ime was running out.

 If it was going to be done, it had to be done right now. In a few minutes, it would be too late. Soon the guests would be moving from the grand lobby toward what was once the ballroom of the mansion, for the auction.

A wide stage had been constructed along one wall and now the scene of so many dances and parties served as a theater and assembly hall. In the middle of the stage was a podium with a microphone. A small table next to the podium held a glass and a pitcher filled with water.

 Now. You've got to do it now.

Donning gloves, mounting the steps, grabbing the pitcher, and taking it behind the curtains at the left side of the stage was done in just seconds. Removing the cyanide from its hiding place, pouring it into the water, and replacing the pitcher on the table took only a few more.

But the short pause to watch the crystals dissolve was a mistake. In those few seconds, a figure with white hair rushed past the entrance to the ballroom.

Chapter 16

The guests began streaming in and selecting the gilded ballroom chairs that were arranged in neat rows facing the stage. Piper took a seat at the back of the room. Phillip Brooks sat a few chairs away.

Piper noticed that Phillip was a little grayer than he was in the photos that had appeared in the New York tabloids at the time of his arrest for embezzlement. There had been no trial. A plea deal had been reached. He had served only a few months in jail but had been ordered to make restitution to the clients he had cheated. Glenna told Piper that it would take years.

Glenna insisted that the marriage had frayed long before her husband got enmeshed in his legal problems. Her theory was that because Phillip was a cheat, he didn't trust others not to cheat as well. Phillip was insanely jealous, wanting to know everything Glenna did and everyone she talked to. Piper remembered Phillip's repeatedly showing up at the soap opera set, as if letting Glenna and everyone else know that he was protecting his "property."

He was constantly accusing Glenna of being romantically involved with her costar. Glenna wasn't, and denied it, but Phillip never believed her.

Glenna had confided in Piper, recounting the jealous rages Phillip flew into at night, fueled by his insecurities—and scotch. Glenna worried about what it was doing to Susannah, yet she hung on, not wanting her daughter to come from a broken home.

The notoriety surrounding Phillip's embezzlement only exacerbated an intolerable marital situation. For their daughter's sake, Glenna was helping him pay back the money he owed his victims. But, in the aftermath of her breakup, Glenna had taken up with Travis York, the man Phillip had accused all along of romancing his wife. The affair hadn't lasted long.

Piper stole a glance at Phillip, who was craning his neck to see the stage. His facial expression was grave and his jaw rippled as he clenched his teeth at the sight of his ex-wife. Glenna, now wearing a red silk dress, was standing at the platform, holding the first item up for bid. Travis adjusted the microphone, wearing his tuxedo with the ease of a man who was confident in his appearance and accomplishments. His rugged good looks and Glenna's sparkling beauty held the attention of every person in the room.

"Good evening, ladies and gentlemen," Travis began, looking around at the audience and flashing a blindingly white grin. "Ready to take out those checkbooks?"

The audience chuckled politely.

"What a good-looking crowd you are," Travis continued, "all ready to bid heartily and generously, knowing that every dollar you spend is going to better the environment in which your daughters are educated."

The applause was enthusiastic but Piper noticed that Phillip Brooks's hands remained still. In spite of herself, she felt sorry for Phillip. He had really made a mess of his life. Once, he had had it all, with a beautiful family and a big job. Now, he was an admitted felon with a broken marriage, his personal and professional life shattered. He had to be miserable.

"Let's hear it, ladies and gentlemen, for one of our most talented parents here at Metropolitan, Miss Martha Killeen. We've all marveled at her work in *Vogue* and *Harper's Bazaar*. There's no one in the world who has more creativity—and not only will she be documenting our event tonight, she has donated her time and talent as one of tonight's auction items."

After the audience finished enthusiastically applaud-
ing, Travis cleared his throat.

"So let's get started," he cheered. "The fabulous
Glenna Brooks is holding up the first item. What do I
hear for the man's TAG Heuer watch?"

One by one, the items listed on the program were
auctioned off as the audience paid rapt attention to the
action on stage, whispering to each other and straining
to see who was paying what for each luxurious item.
Almost $1 million had been raised by the time the
heated bidding began for the photography session with
Martha Killeen.

Piper saw Martha snapping pictures of the audience
and of what was happening onstage. Piper was definitely impressed. It must have been difficult for Martha
to show up in support of the school when everyone and
their mother knew she was going through such a financial nightmare.

"Come on, ladies and gents," Travis urged the bidding upward. "You can go to Martha's studio or she will
come to you. Don't you have a special event coming up
that you'd like to have recorded by the best photographer in the world?"

Eventually, the bidding came down to Quent Raynor
and Glenna, who called out from the stage.

"I bet you want it for your upcoming wedding, don't
you, Glenna?" asked Travis. "Go for it, baby."

Glenna beamed her dazzling smile and gazed out into the audience at her fiancé. He shrugged his shoulders. She closed her eyes and said, "Fifty thousand."

Everyone turned to look at Quent Raynor.

"One hundred thousand dollars," he called out defiantly.

The spectators let out a collective gasp and turned their attention to Glenna and her next move. The actress executed an exaggerated bow to her boss.

"It's all yours," she said.

Chapter 17

I t was a bargain, really. You couldn't put a price tag on all the publicity that would be garnered for *A Little Rain Must Fall* when Martha Killeen worked her magic. Quent was certain that many of the top magazines would be interested in running a story, with Killeen's photos attached. He was thrilled that he had been successful in obtaining the precious prize and confident that he could find a way to pay for it by juggling the *ALRMF* budget.

He knew exactly when he wanted Martha to come to the set: it would be perfect when they shot the dream sequence. Afterward, there would be a few weeks before the show debuted from Los Angeles. During that period, the pictures would get all sorts of play, in print and on the Internet, luring viewers to tune in and watch as the soap opera continued. It could only help the ratings.

As he watched Glenna Brooks walk over to the table next to the podium and pour a glass of water, Quent was happy for another reason. He was glad that he had foiled Glenna by making sure she didn't get the photo shoot she wanted so much. She had been calling all the shots lately, and it angered him. Glenna was acting selfishly, as if her personal life was paramount. What about all the people who needed *A Little Rain Must Fall* to succeed? Their livelihood depended on the show. And for Quent, the show *was* his life.

Glenna was putting his life in jeopardy.

Chapter 18

Following the bidding, Glenna was looking out at the audience as she put down the pitcher. Not paying attention to what she was doing, she misjudged the space on the tabletop and knocked over the glass of water she had just poured.

"Oh, I'm such a klutz," she exclaimed.

Someone rushed out with a roll of paper towels, cleaned up the spill, and took away the broken glass.

"I'm gonna try to get it right this time, folks," said Glenna, smiling as she picked up the pitcher and poured water into the remaining glass.

Glenna was just about to take a sip when Travis turned his head away from the microphone for a spate of coughing.

"Here you go, Travis. Drink this," she said, passing the glass to him.

"I can wait," said Travis unconvincingly.

Another cough.

"Okay, thanks." He turned to the audience. "Hold on a minute, everybody," he said, holding up his index finger. Raising the glass to his lips, Travis took a long gulp, followed by another. He ignored the funny taste. *Maybe it's the building's old pipes,* he thought.

The auctioneer continued to cough. He took another swallow.

"You want to take a break for a few minutes?" whispered Glenna.

"No, I'll be all right."

Travis brought the glass to his mouth again and drank. Afterward, his face reddened and he began to hack uncontrollably. He brought his hand to his forehead.

"Dizzy. I feel dizzy," he sputtered as he staggered forward. "I can't catch my breath." He winced in agony, clutching his stomach.

Glenna reached out as Travis collapsed into her arms. The force of his weight led them both to the floor as someone in the audience shouted, "Call 911!"

Chapter 19

Martha Killeen rushed toward the stage and began taking pictures. Her camera lens captured Glenna fumbling to loosen Travis York's tie and unbuttoning the top of his shirt. Martha took pictures of Travis writhing in agony on the stage floor. As Casey Walden and Quent Raynor climbed onto the stage, Martha turned to take general shots of the audience, who sat filled with horror yet driven to watch what was happening right in front of them.

It took less than ten minutes for the paramedics to arrive, but by then Travis was comatose.

"He's still got a pulse," shouted the emergency worker to his partner.

Martha got pictures of Travis being intubated, as well as shots of Travis, his face a bright cherry-red, being lifted to a stretcher and rolled out of the room.

Piper's first instinct was to move to the stage, but a man identifying himself as a doctor had run up and started administering CPR. She decided to stand aside and not add to the crowd that had gathered.

Thoughts of her father and his emergency preparedness kits flashed through her mind. She wondered if he had anything in them that would have helped Travis York. As it was, Piper cursed herself for changing to her small clutch tonight from her big shoulder bag, which contained the basic kit her father had made her promise to keep with her at all times. This thing was sure to make the news, and Piper knew her dad was going to grill her about what she had done to help.

Even in her state of horror, Piper couldn't help observing that Martha Killeen was taking so many pictures of Travis as he struggled to survive. There was something gross about it. She also noticed that Phillip Brooks had risen to his feet but sat back down again when he saw Casey Walden running to the stage to be with Glenna. In the bedlam of the ballroom, while men shouted and women cried, Piper could feel her heart pounding and the heat rising in her cheeks. She had never before witnessed a man fighting for his life. She feared that Travis York had already lost his battle.

Chapter 20

His wife had long since gone up to bed, ever aware that she had to get up very early in the morning to get to the bakery. Vin Donovan watched the Knicks game in his basement lair while having a couple of beers. When the game was over, he switched to his favorite local news station.

On the television screen, a pretty young woman bundled in a down coat stood on the sidewalk in front of an elegant old building. She held a microphone to her lips with a gloved hand.

"A fund-raising auction at the Metropolitan School for Girls here on Fifth Avenue became the scene of tragedy when actor Travis York collapsed on the stage while he acted as auctioneer. He was later pronounced dead at Lenox Hill Hospital.

"People who attended the auction were stunned and shaken as they left the school tonight, struggling to make sense of what they had witnessed."

Video of a well-dressed couple appeared on the screen. The woman was clinging to the man's arm. Both their facial expressions were grim.

"One minute he was standing there," said the man, "making jokes with the audience, trying to jack up the prices, and the next minute he was coughing and gasping for air. His face was beet-red, almost purple. I could see it from the middle of the room where we were sitting. After he fell to the floor, it looked like he was having a seizure or convulsions or something. He was shaking and jerking around uncontrollably."

Another man appeared and spoke. "I'm still not sure exactly what happened. About halfway through the auction, he coughed a little bit and then he took a drink of water. After that, all hell broke loose."

Vin heard the reporter's voice again. She was talking over a professional head shot of Travis York's handsome face, which smiled from the screen.

"Travis York is known to millions as Drake Darrington on the popular soap opera *A Little Rain Must Fall.* He had volunteered to be the auctioneer tonight at the request of his costar Glenna Brooks, whose daughter attends the school."

Now a woman appeared. The words marching across the bottom of the screen identified her as Jessie Terhune, School Drama Teacher.

"This is just such a horrible, senseless thing," she said. "The man was doing a good deed. The proceeds of the auction are meant to go to the drama department. Travis York, as an actor, knew how important our program is to the girls. Before he collapsed, over a million dollars had already been raised and that is a tribute to him and will be part of his legacy."

The reporter appeared on screen one last time. "An autopsy will be performed. The Office of the Chief Medical Examiner investigates all unexpected, violent, or suspicious deaths in New York City."

Vin lowered the volume on the TV and reached for the phone. He listened in frustration at the repeated ringing before the call was finally transferred to voice mail.

"Piper? It's me. Dad. Are you all right, honey? Call me back as soon as you get this. And whatever you do, don't go near the water that Travis York drank."

Sitting on the old couch, Vin waited anxiously and thought about the news report. The symptoms that the onlookers described reminded him of a couple of cases he'd worked on. Those cases involved cyanide poisoning.

Chapter 21

The police asked for a list of names of those who had attended the auction and questioned all the people remaining in the ballroom. Every single person described the reaction Travis York had after he drank the water. The crime scene investigators confiscated the glass, the pitcher, and the remaining contents for testing.

Glenna was somber as she joined her fiancé and friend after the police had finished interviewing her.

"I still can't believe all this," she said as she sank down in the ballroom chair beside Piper. "I can't believe that Travis is dead." Glenna tilted her head back and closed her eyes.

"I know," said Casey, taking her hand and bringing it to his lips. "But what I can't believe is how close it came to being you, Glenna. You almost drank that water instead of Travis."

"Casey's right," said Piper. "Thank God that didn't happen."

"I do thank him," said Glenna. "But we don't know for certain that it was something in that water that killed Travis."

"I overheard one of the cops talking," said Piper. "That's what they're thinking."

Glenna straightened in her chair. "So somebody poisoned Travis?" she asked incredulously. "Why in the world would anyone do that?"

"I don't know," said Piper, shaking her head. "But here's the thing, Glenna: if it does turn out that the water was poisoned, what if it was really meant for you?"

Glenna looked at Piper with skepticism. "No way," she said.

"It could have been," said Piper. "And maybe it has something to do with that letter you got."

"What letter?" asked Casey.

Glenna shook her head. "I didn't even want to tell you about it. Nonsense, that's all it was. I burned it."

"You've got to tell Casey about it, Glenna," said Piper. "And now you have to tell the police about it, too."

Chapter 22

Martha Killeen had followed the paramedics out onto Fifth Avenue, taking pictures until the body of Travis York was loaded into the back of the ambulance. Then she hailed a cab and directed the driver to take her downtown to her studio. As she sat in the back of the taxi, Martha scrolled through the photos that appeared in the playback viewer of her camera.

The pictures were powerful and graphic. Martha was well aware of the fact that, because she had taken them, they were more valuable. Even if somebody had taken some pictures with their cell phones, they weren't going to be in any way comparable to hers in terms of clarity, composition, and pedigree. The photographs she had taken tonight were worth a fortune.

The appetite for the pictures was going to be tremendous. Once word got out that she had them, broadcast and Internet news agencies would be after her like voracious hounds. She had to decide how she was going to handle things.

Martha ran her fingers through her short, layered hair as she considered her options. She could sell the whole series of pictures to a single buyer, an exclusive arrangement that would net one enormous sum of money. She could sell to multiple buyers and possibly make even more. Or she could let the pictures out one or two at a time and try to stretch things out, choosing buyers based on their offers for a particular picture.

But she also had the police to consider. Once they learned of the pictures she had taken, they might confiscate them as part of their investigation. Then she'd have nothing.

She had to act quickly.

The cab pulled up in front of her building. Martha paid the fare, got out, and stood on the sidewalk in front of the old three-story warehouse that she had so passionately renovated into her 13,000-square-foot studio and living space. Just Martha and her six-year-old daughter, Ella, shared five bedrooms, five baths, three fireplaces, and an indoor lap pool. Outside, at the back of the building, there were another 2,000 square feet of multilevel terraces and gardens. With her studio on the first floor, Martha literally lived over the store, and was available for Ella whenever needed.

A place like hers was almost nonexistent in Manhattan—though it really wasn't hers at all. Three different banks held mortgages on it now. Still, the thought of losing it sickened her. It was the only home Ella had ever known—except, of course, for the Chinese orphanage. Ella was doing so well here and Martha didn't want to disrupt that. Her daughter had already been through enough in her short life.

Some people would argue that she didn't need to live so lavishly, that Ella didn't need to go to a private school. But Martha was determined to give her child the best of everything.

As she straightened the wreath on the front door, Martha made her decision.

Chapter 23

Friday, December 10 . . .
Fourteen days until the wedding

B efore he drank his morning coffee or turned on his computer to monitor what the overseas financial markets had done overnight, Phillip Brooks bundled up for the three-block walk to the nearest newsstand. He didn't have a subscription to the *New York Post,* but he suspected that the paper would have the most gripping coverage of what had happened last night. If there were pictures to be had, the *Post* would use them liberally, splashing them across the front page and throughout the tabloid. Going to the Internet was no substitute for holding a newspaper in your own hands.

He locked the door of his junior one-bedroom apartment and took the elevator down three floors to the small reception area where the building's residents picked up their mail from the metal boxes set into the wall. As Phillip reached to open the heavy glass door that led out to the street, he was nostalgic for the days when he took a doorman for granted, the days when he and Glenna had lived together in the luxurious "classic eight," the apartment that Glenna lived in now with Susannah. It sickened him that, soon, Casey Walden would live there, too.

It was all he could do to nod and keep a pleasant expression on his face when Susannah mentioned things that she did with her mother and future stepfather. Every other weekend, Phillip had to listen to Susannah's account of the latest excursion she had gone on with Glenna and Casey. The guy was a regular tour guide, taking them to the Museum of Natural History, the Bronx Zoo, the New York Aquarium, and always finding other interesting outings. A walking tour of Greenwich Village, where Casey told her about the many writers and artists who had lived there over the decades; a picnic on the grounds of the Cloisters, where he expounded on the highlights of medieval art; a boat ride out to Ellis Island, where Susannah was able to find the listing for her maternal great-great-grandparents who had arrived in the United States after a miserable ocean voyage from Ireland.

Phillip knew he should be glad that the man who aimed to be Susannah's stepfather was the sort that seemed to enjoy spending time with his daughter, doing such wholesome and educational things. But all Phillip could feel was jealousy and resentment and anger.

Casey Walden was stealing his life.

Reaching the newsstand, Phillip picked up the newspaper and stared at the glaring image of Travis York lying on the stage floor, his mouth gaping open, his eyes bulging. He noticed that a photo credit was given to Martha Killeen. As Phillip studied the picture further, he was surprised at how little emotion he felt. Once he had been so jealous of Travis that he couldn't sleep at night. He had been tortured by thoughts of Travis and Glenna being together. He had been certain that, despite Glenna's denials, Travis had played a big part in the dissolution of their marriage. Phillip had been consumed by his hatred for the man.

Now all Phillip felt was a sense of satisfaction. Travis York had deserved what he had gotten. Coveting another man's wife was a sin.

Now, at least, half of Phillip's competition was out of the way.

Chapter 24

Her blond hair fanned out on the pillow, Piper awoke to the smell of coffee drifting up from the kitchen and Emmett licking her face. She stretched and took in a deep breath, staring at the bubble-gum-pink walls and wishing she had gotten involved in picking this paint color. Then she remembered. Travis York had died last night. Even worse, there was a good chance he might have been murdered.

Instinctively reaching for her BlackBerry, Piper scrolled around, looking for the latest news. She read, paying close attention to every word. There was nothing in any of the stories about Travis York's death that she hadn't known last night when she left the auction. But the police were scheduled to hold a news conference later in the day.

This was one morning she didn't have to rack her brain for something to post. Piper began pecking at her handheld's keyboard, typing an entry for all those following her on Twitter, careful not to exceed the 140-character limit.

I WAS AMONG THE VERY LAST PEOPLE WHO SAW TRAVIS YORK ALIVE. HE WAS SO TALENTED. ALWAYS KIND TO ME. HE WILL BE SORELY MISSED BY 1000s OF FANS.

Laying the BlackBerry on the bedside table, Piper went to the bathroom and brushed her teeth. She turned on the water in the shower, waited for it to spray hot, and then stepped into the stall. She let the water run over her body, soothing the tension she felt. Her hair was full of shampoo lather when her phone buzzed.

Jack Lombardi waited impatiently for Piper to answer. After four rings, voice mail sprang into action. Frustrated, Jack left his message.

"Pipe? It's me. I just read your tweet. If you told me you were going to be at that auction, I'd forgotten. I want to talk to you, Pipe. To make sure you're okay and to eat some humble pie. I was sure that Glenna's letter was from a harmless crank. But now that I hear that Glenna could have just as easily taken a drink from that pitcher, I'm thinking maybe someone really has it in for her and that the letter could be a strong clue.

"Oh, yeah, they were able to determine that there was cyanide in the water. They suspected cyanide and checked specifically for that right away. But that's not for publication yet. Anyway, that letter has to make its way to the police."

As she went down to the kitchen to pour herself a glass of orange juice, Piper heard the familiar banging coming from the basement. The sound of her father's tinkering was oddly soothing to her. It had always been this way.

Piper remembered coming home after a Friday night out with friends in high school. While she had never admitted it, Piper was nervous when she was in a car with a friend who drove too fast or at a party where people drank themselves into blackouts.

Even though she knew he was still up just to make sure she was home by her curfew, the sound of her father at his workbench never failed to remind her that she was safe. That she was home.

Sense memory at its best.

She carried her drink with her downstairs. She found her father rummaging through an old applesauce jar containing odd nails and screws. He put it down immediately when he heard her.

"Hi, Dad."

"What time did you finally get home last night?"

"I don't know. I guess it was after one."

"It was after two. I heard you."

"Then why are you asking me?"

Vin shrugged. "Force of habit, I guess. I left you a message and you didn't call me back."

"By the time I noticed it, I was afraid you'd be asleep and I didn't want to wake you."

Vin seemed to accept the explanation. "All right. Tell me about what you saw."

Piper closed her eyes. "It was a horror show, Dad."

"Death by poison usually is," said Vin, "if that's what it turns out to be."

"It *was* poison," said Piper. "Cyanide. Jack Lombardi just left me a message about it."

"The FBI kid?"

Piper nodded. "Somehow I don't think Jack would appreciate being referred to as 'the FBI kid.'"

"He's a kid to me," said Vin.

"Whatever."

"Actually, I'm not surprised the detectives suspected cyanide. It's a great poison," Vin continued. "It looks like sugar, can be dissolved in water or hidden in food or medications. Except for the smell of bitter almonds, there's really nothing that warns you until it's too late. And I read somewhere that being able to detect the almond scent is a genetic thing. Some people can, some people can't."

Piper sank into the worn sofa. "Cyanide. It's so dramatic. It's like *Masterpiece Theatre* on Fifth Avenue."

"It's not really all that exotic, Piper," said Vin as he found the nail he wanted. "We had a couple of cyanide poisoning cases while I was on the force. All three involved somebody who was ticked off with a husband, wife, or former lover. And, of course, there were those famous cases in the early eighties when some idiot was going around lacing extra-strength Tylenol capsules with cyanide. If I remember correctly, seven people were killed by that animal."

"Did they ever find out who did it?" asked Piper.

"They've had a couple of suspects but they've never had enough evidence to charge any of them with murder." Vin began vigorously hitting the nail with his hammer.

"Where do you even *get* cyanide?" asked Piper when there was a pause in the pounding.

"It's not all that hard to buy, lovey," said Vin as he took out his measuring tape. "It's available for commercial use and mainly produced for mining gold and silver. It's used in electroplating and cleaning metal. Labs use it as a reducing agent and it's also used as an insecticide. I remember in one of our cases, the killer's hobby was collecting bugs. He used potassium cyanide to euthanize his insects . . . and then his wife."

Piper winced. "Wow. There's a winner."

"And here's another reason not to smoke. Cyanide has been found in cigarettes."

"Lovely."

Chapter 25

The decision was made not to hold classes at the Metropolitan School for Girls the day following the auction. Parents were alerted by robo-call. However, teachers were expected to attend a morning meeting where a psychologist would address them on how to handle the subject of Travis York's death with the students when they came back to school on Monday.

Jessie Terhune sat amid her colleagues and listened, seemingly absorbed in what the psychologist was saying. But she was distracted. Casey Walden was sitting in the row in front of her. Jessie had to concentrate to keep her eyes on the speaker when all she really wanted to do was look at Casey.

She still loved him. It was torture to know that he loved somebody else.

After the psychologist answered questions from the audience, Michele Cox, the headmistress, came up to the stage and thanked him. Then Mrs. Cox addressed the teachers herself.

"I just thought that you should also know that, thanks to Travis York, the auction was a huge success. Before he was stricken, our auctioneer cajoled over a million dollars from our audience. And this morning, we have been getting calls and e-mails from people all around the country who would like to donate to a fund benefiting our school drama department in his memory."

So it had worked, thought Jessie, determined to keep her facial expression solemn. Speaking to the reporters in front of the school last night had done just what she had hoped it would. Suggesting that Travis York supported her drama department was spurring on his fans. Who knew how many people would donate because they wanted to pay tribute to Travis!

Casey turned around and gave her a sad smile. Jessie tried to read it. Was he happy that her department was going to reap a windfall but appropriately melancholy because of the circumstances? Or was his face expressing pity for her because he knew that she still loved him?

Suddenly, Jessie felt self-conscious, aware that she had more than a few gray hairs, her lipstick had worn off, and her boxy suit jacket was four years old.

How frumpy I must look to him, in comparison to Glenna.

But Jessie smiled back, determined not to give him the satisfaction of thinking that she cared about him at all. Let him think that she had moved on, that she was focused on her beloved work. Wait until he saw the dynamic direction her drama department would take now.

Nothing is over yet, Casey, she thought, holding on to a hope that they might still have some future together. *You can never tell what's going to happen next. It could have just as easily been your precious Glenna as Travis York last night.*

Life was unpredictable.

Chapter 26

Everyone was clearly shaken. There were tears and blank expressions and faces contorted in grief as the actors and crew arrived on the set of *A Little Rain Must Fall*. Despite Travis's death, the show was going on. There was a taping schedule that had to be met.

Quent gathered the staff together in a rehearsal hall. As he waited for everyone to find a place to sit, he took off his glasses and rubbed his eyes and the bridge of his nose. He cleared his throat and replaced his glasses before starting to speak.

"First of all, I want to thank all of you for coming at what is, for all of us, a terribly sad and absolutely horrific time. Travis's death is a profound loss. He was an incredibly talented actor with a charismatic personality. He was a treasured colleague and friend to all of us.

"Just a few minutes ago, I took a call from the police, a courtesy call really, with news that they will reveal later in the day. They have ascertained that the water Travis drank was laced with cyanide."

Some gasped, some mumbled to those sitting beside them, all of them shook their heads as they struggled to comprehend the idea that the man who had been with them, taping a scene not even twenty-four hours before, had been murdered.

Quent paused and scanned his audience. After several moments, he continued speaking.

"Distasteful as it may be, we have to figure out how Travis's death will impact the show. The writers and I will gather as soon as we finish here to figure out what to do with the scripts. Once it's decided how we'll explain what happened to Travis's character, we'll figure out what previously taped scenes have to be amended and what new scenes will be needed to advance our story line. In the meantime, there are some scenes that have nothing to do with Travis's character that can still be taped as scheduled. So, everyone, let's take one day at a time and do the best we can. Let's do Travis proud."

Quent looked appropriately somber as he finished speaking. Of course, he hadn't expressed *all* of his thoughts and feelings.

From a business point of view, it would have been better if Glenna had been the one to die. A Little Rain Must Fall was losing her anyway. But, then again, even Travis's dying was incredible publicity.

Chapter 27

Arthur Walden and his wife, Laura, sat in tufted leather wing chairs in the office on the top floor of the Madison Avenue building that housed Walden's Jewelers. They watched the story about the soap opera star's death on Channel 2's *News at Noon*. There were two sound bites from the police press conference in the piece, one declaring that Travis York had died of cyanide poisoning, the other asking that anyone with information pertinent to the case come forward and assist the investigation.

At the conclusion of the story, Arthur clicked off the television and turned to his wife.

"It could have just as easily gone the other way," he said. "This tragedy could have struck much closer to home. It could have been Glenna."

Laura rested her head on the back of the chair and closed her eyes. "I know," she said. "Thank God it wasn't. Can you imagine how Casey would have taken that?"

"He would have been devastated," said Arthur as he stood up. "But it wasn't Glenna. Casey can go on with his plans."

Laura's head snapped forward at the change in tone of her husband's voice. She glared at him. "You know you could sound happier about it, Arthur. Casey is your brother and he's been single all his life. You should be glad that he's finally found someone he wants to settle down with."

"It's not that I don't want Casey to be happy, Laura," said Arthur. "What I can't stand is the fact that all of a sudden he wants to stick his nose in the business. I'm not used to that and I don't want it."

"You've been spoiled, Arthur," said Laura. "We've been spoiled. Never having to answer to anyone, Casey accepting whatever you told him, whatever yearly dividend you sent him. It was naive to think it could go on forever like that. The business was left to the both of you."

"But I've done all the work," said Arthur.

"And you've compensated yourself well for it."

Arthur began to speak, but thought better of it. Not even Laura knew how well he had paid himself. And if his brother ever found out and demanded that he make restitution—or, worse, filed criminal charges—Arthur would be ruined.

Chapter 28

The outside air was cold, the gusting winds made trees and bushes sway, and the forecast was for snow—but Piper was dressed in sandals and wore spandex shorts under her sweatpants as she drove her parents' car toward the center of town. She was cutting it close. If she was late, the door would be locked and she wouldn't be able to take her class.

As Piper pulled into a parking space in front of the yoga studio, her BlackBerry sounded. Before answering, she glanced to see who was calling. She hoped that it was someone who could wait. But when she saw it was her agent, she pushed the ACCEPT key.

"Hey, Gabe. What's up?"

"I'm fine, Piper. How are you?" He was being sarcastic.

"Sorry about that," said Piper. Whenever Gabe called, Piper hoped it would be good news, but today all she wanted was for him to be brief. This was the latest yoga class, and Piper was dying for the workout. Thankfully, he didn't take long.

"*A Little Rain Must Fall,* Monday. You can phone in for your call time. It should be posted by now. Do you still have the number?"

"Yeah, I do. What about the script? Can they e-mail it to me, or do I have to go to the studio to pick it up?"

"It's in flux, Piper. The writers are going to be working all weekend trying to figure out how to adapt to losing Travis. They'll send the lines as soon as they have them."

The first thing that struck Piper was the familiar stench. It was pungent and unpleasant. Still, it smelled a lot better than the place she frequented in New York.

Any Bikram yoga studio she had ever visited had a bad odor. A group of people exercising in a room heated to 105 degrees Fahrenheit, with the humidity at 40 percent, produced gallons of sweat. The idea was to keep the body warm and sweating profusely. It helped get rid of toxins and allowed the body to be more flexible.

Some yogis didn't like Bikram, because it didn't stress the meditation aspect of yoga. It was primarily a workout. That was precisely why Piper was a loyal fan. She tried to go four or even five times a week, and she always made it to at least three sessions—unlike her karate refresher classes, which she only took from time to time. Her father insisted she keep up the skills she had begun acquiring when she was eleven years old— also at his insistence. Vin Donovan wanted his daughter to be able to defend herself.

Fluorescent lights blazed from the ceiling. Piper tried to keep her eyes open and focused on the image of herself in the mirror, not looking at the other students, listening only to the commands of the instructor. But Piper was distracted. The murder, her return to the soap, even the realization that there were only two weeks until Glenna and Casey's wedding, kept her mind spinning. She had no definite plans about what the wedding cake should be, but Piper knew two things: it had to make Glenna happy and it had to make Piper look good.

After an hour and a half in the hot room, twisting into cobra, locust, tree, eagle, and camel postures, Piper's body glistened with perspiration. She wiped herself with a towel, rolled up her yoga mat, pulled on her sweats, and hurried out to the car in the cold. On the way home, she stopped at the CVS in downtown Hill-wood, ignoring the stares of other customers as they watched the young woman with a red face and sweat-soaked hair that was practically still steaming. Piper headed for the magazine racks and pulled off copies of *Brides* and *Martha Stewart Weddings*.

Then she caught sight of the newspaper headlines.

GOING, GOING, GONE! blasted one of the tab-loids in inch-high letters over a photo of Travis York's body cradled in Glenna Brooks's arms.

TRAVIS YORK TAKES FINAL BOW! announced another insensitively.

The feeling of well-being she had at the end of the yoga class morphed into tension as visions of Travis writhing on the stage came into her head. She felt her chest tighten. *Get it together, Piper,* she told herself. *Breathe. Breathe.*

She needed to *do* something. Taking action would make her feel better. She wanted to help in the criminal investigation, but how? She had already racked her memory for anything she might have noticed last night at the auction and had come up empty. She wished she had forced Jack to analyze that threatening letter that Glenna had received. Now, the note was only ashes in the Metropolitan School for Girls' fireplace. It was so frustrating.

Until the writers finished, she couldn't even put her energy into studying her script. But there was something constructive she *could* do. She knew she'd feel much better if she did something about designing the wedding cake.

Tomorrow she was going to spend time in the bakery, brushing up on her decorating skills. And she'd also promised to help her mother with a new commercial over the weekend. In the meantime, Piper grabbed the tabloids, added them to her magazines, and carried them all to the register.

On Fridays, the Donovans ate pizza.

Piper still loved pizza night—it never got old. It had been happening since her parents were kids. The Catholic Church had placed a ban on eating meat on Fridays. Piper had heard that the ban had very little to do with religion and everything to do with a struggling fish industry. And even though the Church had lifted the ban before Piper was born, the pizza tradition happily lived on.

Piper stopped at Pompilio's on the way home and ordered a large tomato-and-cheese pie. While she waited, she perused the newspapers. Looking at the picture of Travis York sprawled on the stage floor, she noticed that a photo credit was given to Martha Killeen.

Inside, there was a sidebar story recounting the fact that Killeen had been at the auction and had taken the exclusive pictures. Many of the haunting photos she had taken were splashed across the inner pages of the paper. The other newspaper had a theatrical head shot of Travis on the front page, with some grainier shots of the auction action inside. Piper assumed they had been taken with cell phones.

The sidebar didn't mention how much Martha Killeen had been paid for her pictures, but Piper suspected it would be in the six figures somewhere, maybe even more. Not a bad dividend from a charity event.

By seven o'clock, the pizza had been eaten, the dishes had been washed, and her parents were settled in for an evening of television. After going through the bridal magazines, Piper wasn't sure what to do with herself. A book? A bath?

Was this what her twenty-seven-year-old life had come to?

She pounced on her BlackBerry when she heard it ring.

"Pipe. It's me."

"Hi, Me."

"What are you doing?"

"Please. I wonder that every minute of every day."

"Did you get in touch with Glenna?" asked Jack. "Did she turn that letter over to the P.D.?"

"Uh-uh," answered Piper. "There is no letter."

"What do you mean?"

"When I told her you didn't think it was anything to worry about, she threw it in the fireplace and burned it."

"Crap."

"I know," Piper responded.

"I'm sorry, Pipe. I was sure that thing was from some crackpot."

Piper didn't say anything.

"The silence is deafening, Piper," said Jack. "Give me a break will you? I feel terrible about this."

"Don't worry about it, Jack. We don't know for sure that the letter had anything to do with the murder. But doesn't it seem like more than a coincidence that Glenna would get a letter like that and then Travis is killed? That poison could have just as easily been meant for Glenna."

Chapter 29

Sunday, December 12 . . .
Twelve days until the wedding

"E ight-letter word for thorn in one's side," said Casey. "Begins with an N."

Glenna stopped attending to a pile of accumulated mail, got up from her desk, and walked across her apartment's large living room. She sat on the sofa next to her fiancé and studied the puzzle.

"Nuisance?" she suggested.

"Yes. That's it," said Casey, filling in the empty spaces.

"Sweetheart?" asked Glenna as she put her hand up to caress his cheek.

"Um-hmm." Casey didn't look up from the puzzle.

"I've been thinking I should have gone higher."

"Higher for what?" he asked, still focused on the crossword clues.

"For the photo session with Martha Killeen."

That got Casey's attention. He looked at her with an incredulous expression on his face.

"You'd actually be willing to pay over a hundred thousand dollars to have that woman take your picture?" he asked.

"*Our* pictures," Glenna gently corrected him. "Pictures of the day we start our marriage, the happiest day in our lives." Glenna turned and stared at the flames dancing in the fireplace. Her eyes moistened.

Casey put down the magazine and pencil. He pulled Glenna close. "What else is bothering you?" he asked, kissing the top of her head.

"Travis. I just can't believe he's dead."

"I know he meant a great deal to you, sweetheart. I'm so sorry."

They said nothing else as he held her.

The sweet-potato casserole and chicken were roasting in the oven, the table was set, and Casey was helping Susannah with her science project. With a half hour until dinner would be ready, Glenna went back to her desk and the mail. One by one, she opened envelopes. She tossed some, wrote checks for others, and put aside the ones that couldn't be responded to until later. When she neared the bottom of the pile, Glenna inhaled sharply.

She recognized the envelope.

Chapter 30

L ame, Mom," said Piper when she finished reading the little script that Terri had put together for the commercial. "This is lame."

"It is *not* lame," insisted Terri. "With Emmett doing his part, it will be adorable." She held up a cookie and the dog rose up on his hind legs, holding the pose until Terri gave him the reward.

Piper recited the words on the page, bringing her voice to a high pitch. "'The treats at The Icing on the Cupcake Bakery will make you sit up and beg.' Really, Mom? It's so cheesy."

"When you say it like that, of course it sounds ridiculous," said Terri, snatching the paper from Piper's hand. "Never mind, Piper. You don't have to help. I'll do it myself."

Instantly, Piper regretted that she had made fun of her mother's idea. After all, they weren't staging Shakespeare. They were shooting a homemade commercial for a local bakery, starring a dog. And who was Piper to be a critic? Everyone who saw the commercials loved them. More important, her mother took pride in making them.

"I'm sorry, Mom."

Terri didn't say anything.

"That was bratty of me."

"It was." Terri's face broke into a smile. "And now that you've admitted it, let's go ahead and shoot this baby. You handle the camera and I'll do the tricks with Emmett."

"I thought you liked to do the camera work so much," said Piper. "You never want anybody else to touch it."

"Not anymore. Now that you're home, that can be one of your jobs."

"One of my *jobs*?"

"Um-hmm. Don't you think everyone has to pitch in and help around here?"

Piper nodded, knowing her mother was right, but not exactly relishing the idea. "What else do you want me to do?" she asked.

"For one, your father and I think you should take over with the vacuuming. It has to be done every day, you know."

"Good ol' Emmett and your constant shedding," said Piper as she bent down and scratched the terrier behind the ear. "Thanks, Em. Thanks a lot."

Chapter 31

Monday, December 13 . . .
Eleven days until the wedding

She knew she should probably take mass transit to save money, but Piper didn't want to deal with the hassle on her first day. Her mother was lending Piper her car.

Concerned about road conditions, she left home extra early to drive into Manhattan. She arrived twenty minutes before her call time, carrying a box containing more than enough gingerbread men to share with the entire cast and crew. She was nervous. Not only was this her first acting job in quite a while, but her lines had only been e-mailed to her the night before. Piper had stayed up late going over them, trying to commit the words to memory. She didn't have them down yet.

Roosevelt, the beloved security guard, was in his booth at the entrance to the Midtown studio, there to greet and screen, as he had been every day for the last fifteen years.

"Good to see you again, Miss Donovan." He smiled, checking his clipboard. "You are in dressing room 16."

"You don't know how great that sounds to me, Roosevelt," said Piper, smiling back. She opened the bakery box and held the lid open. The aroma of gingerbread burst from the container. "Help yourself," she said.

He reached in and took one, smiling as he noticed that the gingerbread man had ALRMF piped in icing on its chest.

"Thank you, miss."

"You're welcome," said Piper. "Take another."

Dressing room 16 was at the end of a long hallway. Piper was thrilled to see MISS DONOVAN posted next to the door. Inside, the room was a small box, dominated by a large mirror, rimmed with round lightbulbs, on one wall and a big closet on the other. A makeup table in front of the mirror, chair, and chaise longue were the only furnishings. Piper couldn't have been happier had she been at Versailles.

Piper laid the bakery box on the makeup table and took off her coat. Opening the closet door, she took a deep breath as she saw the three white evening gowns hanging there. Piper separated the dresses so she could get a better look. Each one was gorgeous.

Oh, man, I've missed this. It's so wonderful to be back!

There was a soft knock on the dressing-room door.

"Come in," said Piper as she reached for the knob.

A middle-aged woman with close-cropped white hair and warm hazel eyes stood in the doorway. Piper noticed that the skin beneath her eyes was red and puffy and her porcelainlike skin was blotchy.

"Peggy," cried Piper, opening her arms and grinning. "It's so great to see you."

The women embraced.

"It's been too long," said Peggy as she pulled back, her eyes searching Piper's face. "How's everything?"

People automatically asked that question, but Piper knew that Peggy actually wanted to hear the answer.

"In a nutshell, haven't been getting much acting work and moved back in with my parents for a while," said Piper. "How sorry is that?"

"It's not easy," said Peggy.

"And what about you?" asked Piper.

Peggy's mouth turned down at the corners. "I'm not moving out to the West Coast with the show because my parents aren't doing so well and I don't want to be that far away from them. I don't have another job yet, but God is good and I know something will turn up. What really has me thrown, though, is what happened to Travis. I can't stop crying about it. When I think I was right there. . . ." Her voice trailed off.

"You were at the auction last night?" asked Piper. "I didn't see you."

Peggy nodded. "Glenna called me at the last minute and asked me to come with another dress. I rushed in and out pretty quickly, but I grabbed a copy of the program on the way out. It was very impressive. In fact, I was going through it again just this morning."

The wardrobe mistress straightened resolutely. "Well, let's get to what we have to do," she said. "The show must go on and all that."

Peggy took one of the garments out of the closet and handed it to Piper. "The script calls for all the characters in the dream sequence to be dressed in white. I still had your measurements on file, Piper, so all three of these should fit you. Start trying them on. Let's see which one looks best."

After it was decided that the white dupioni-silk asymmetrical gown was the one, Peggy took the dress away to alter the hem. Piper put on a robe and settled down on the chaise. She pulled the script from her bag and began to go over lines while she waited to be called.

After forty-five minutes, Piper decided to go out to the set and see if she could gauge how long it would be until they would be ready for her scene.

Within the cavernous space, an entire world had been created. The *Little Rain* studio contained a doctor's office, a nurse's station, and hospital operating and waiting rooms. There were sets for the interior of a chapel, a bar, a delicatessen, a classroom, a pharmacy, and the ballroom of a country club. In storage rooms and hallways adjacent to the studio were carefully marked cartons and bins containing the contents of the bedrooms, kitchens, and living areas of the various houses and apartments of the characters on the show, along with flats that could be rolled in and out to assemble the walls of the fictional dwellings.

The studio was bustling with activity, much of it taking place in the country club ballroom where stagehands were feverishly decorating. In the middle of the set, silver tinsel was being draped on a tall, white Christmas tree with hundreds of clear lights twinkling from its branches. All of the tables and chairs in the ballroom were covered in white, and swags of white garland hung from the crystal chandeliers. Other workers were beginning to cover the floor with artificial snow.

There was none of the usual banter as the stagehands went about their jobs. The studio was eerily quiet. Travis York's death was on everyone's mind.

From the information she had gotten the night before, Piper knew that this was to be the scene for the dream that Glenna's character, Maggie Lane, was going to have. Before Travis's murder, the plan had been to kill off only Maggie, since Glenna was leaving the show. Now, both Glenna's and Travis York's characters were dying. The white dream sequence was going to wrap it all up and would feature Maggie's dead sister, Mariah, played by Piper.

The story line had been amended to include an explosion that would injure and kill some of the daytime drama characters. Glenna's and Travis's characters would be among the dead. Travis immediately, Glenna hanging on for a while. It was while Glenna, aka Maggie Lane, was unconscious that she would have the dream in which her dead sister appears to her.

Piper was admiring the stagehands' work when she noticed that Quent Raynor had entered. Hands on hips, Quent squinted as he perused the set. The area got noticeably quieter while everyone waited for his reaction.

"It's still not glamorous enough," Quent proclaimed, taking off his glasses and rubbing the bridge of his nose. "It needs more glitz."

Chapter 32

Walden's was within walking distance of the Metropolitan School for Girls. During his lunch period, Casey made his way on the shoveled sidewalks one block over and a few blocks down, entering the elegant storefront on Madison Avenue. A security guard was stationed just inside the door.

"Hiya, Joe," said Casey. He cupped his hands and blew on them. "It's cold out there."

"Hello, Mr. Walden."

"My brother around?"

"Yes, sir. He's downstairs."

"Thanks, Joe." Casey strode through the luxurious showroom, passing velvet-lined display cases containing exquisitely designed necklaces, bracelets, and earrings twinkling with diamonds, rubies, emeralds, and sapphires. He noticed there was easily more sales staff behind the cases than there were customers on the other side. Casey rationalized that Mondays were always slow.

The elevator took him down one floor to the work-rooms. Six artisans were bent over well-lit jewelers' benches. Four of them worked on pieces that would find their way upstairs to the display cases in the showroom. The other two artisans fashioned specially ordered pieces, filling specific requests made by customers in advance.

The room led to another space, where tables supported a lathe, a grinder, a polisher, hammers, casting equipment, and a sonic cleaner. There was also a separate ventilated soldering room and an area where large rectangular tanks were outfitted for electroplating gold and silver. Containers of chemicals were carefully lined up on shelves along one wall.

Casey found Arthur watching as a shining silver teapot was pulled from one of the tanks.

"Can you imagine?" asked Arthur after the brothers shook hands. "This teapot is old, Victorian. Its beauty lay not only in the graceful and ornate design, but in the patina it had acquired over the last century. Yet its owner, who actually bought it at an antique show, mind you, wants it to look like new. I told her she was ruining both the aesthetic and monetary value of the piece. She didn't care."

"Just goes to show that money doesn't buy taste," said Casey.

"True enough," huffed Arthur. "Some of the people moving in around here are making money hand over fist but you should see the things they order. Dripping with stones, but not in a good way."

"I didn't think that would be a problem for you," said Casey.

"Oh, I don't mind selling as much as I can; it offends me if the stones aren't set off artfully and with taste. The gaudy things some people want are repulsive." Arthur shook his head in disgust.

"I want to talk to you about something, Arthur."

"Shoot."

"Privately."

"Don't mind me," said the electroplate technician. "I'm going to lunch."

"Have a seat, Casey," said Arthur, waving to a couple of metal chairs.

"I'll get right to the point," said Casey as he sat. "I could use a hundred thousand."

"Dollars?" asked Arthur. "So could I."

"I mean it, Arthur. The wedding is coming up and I need the money."

"I'm not in a position to take it out of the business accounts right now," Arthur said seriously. "Times are tight, Casey."

"I thought you just told me that all your nouveau riche customers are buying up a storm." Outwardly calm, Casey stared at the shelves on the wall. Inside, he was seething. "Let's get it out in the open, Arthur," he said. "You don't want me to marry Glenna. You don't even like her."

"That's ridiculous," said Arthur. "Of course I like her. Why else do you think I'd go to the trouble of packing up a case of diamonds for her?"

Casey was puzzled. "I don't get it. What are you talking about?"

"I got a call this morning from the guy who runs Glenna's soap opera."

"Quent Raynor?"

"Yes. He asked if Walden's would lend him diamonds for a special finale scene they're doing for Glenna before she leaves the show. I agreed to have the diamonds there on Friday," said Arthur. "Believe me, I wouldn't go to the trouble if it wasn't for Glenna."

"Thank you," said Casey, slightly mollified. "But I still need that hundred grand."

"May I ask why?"

"Not that it's any of your business, but Glenna has her heart set on having Martha Killeen photograph our wedding. I want to make that happen. Actually, I should be asking for more. I'm going to have more expenses when I'm married and I have no intention of being a kept man."

Arthur sighed deeply. "All right," he said. "But you have to promise me that's it for a while."

Casey shook his head. "I'm not going to promise anything of the kind, Arthur. All these years, I've only taken that small stipend from the business when I was entitled to much more. That was fine with me then, but it's not now. Going forward, I have to get what's mine."

Chapter 33

Word spread that there was no chance the dream sequence would be shot that day. Quent was said to be making arrangements to add something to the scene. There would, however, be some dry blocking after lunch.

The free hours were fine with Piper. She used them to catch up with colleagues. She learned who had moved, what great vacations people had taken, and that there were three new babies born to crew members since the last time she had been on the show. But most of the conversations began and ended with expressions of disbelief that Travis York had been murdered and agreement that missing his funeral, scheduled for the next day, would be unthinkable.

Mid-morning, Piper knocked on the door of Glenna's dressing room.

"Come on in."

Piper opened the door and gasped. Glenna stood in the middle of the room, wearing the most beautiful dress that Piper had ever seen. It was a floor-length gown made of ivory embroidered-silk satin organza. The off-the-shoulder, pleated V-neck bodice led to Glenna's tiny waist, and below that was a flowing skirt of cascading petal ruffles. The effect almost made it seem as if Glenna was standing in the clouds.

"What do you think?" asked Glenna, holding her arms out.

"I think you should never take that off," said Piper. "You look absolutely gorgeous! Like a fairy princess, a fantasy."

"Or a soon-to-be-dead soap opera character," Glenna said. "How nice to be wearing a Monique Lhuillier gown on your deathbed." She smiled as she looked at her reflection in the full-length mirror. "You got to give it to Quent. He's pulling out all the stops on this one. My last bow is going to be a memorable one."

While Glenna changed out of the dress, Piper brought up the subject of the wedding cake.

"I know it's crazy to talk about this with everything that's going on, Glenna, but I have some questions to ask you before finalizing the design."

"I thought you wanted to talk to Casey and me together."

"I did," said Piper. "But, if it's all right with you, we'd better go ahead and do it now. The wedding is rapidly approaching. We can call Casey if there's anything he really needs to be consulted on."

"You're right," said Glenna. "And anyway, Casey couldn't care less about the wedding cake. He just wants me to be satisfied. So, go ahead. Shoot."

"Great," said Piper, taking a small spiral notebook out of her robe pocket. "First of all, how many guests?"

"It looks like there will be about a hundred," answered Glenna. "No more than that."

"Perfect," said Piper. *I'll be able to handle it,* she thought.

"Okay. Let's talk about the part that everybody sees on the outside. Do you have any preferences on the color of the icing?"

"I don't know." Glenna shrugged. "White?"

"Sure. We could do that if you want," said Piper. "Are you wearing a white dress?"

"Actually, I thought I'd be wearing an ice-blue silk suit I bought, since this is my second marriage." Glenna nodded toward the gown she had just taken off. "But now, I'm thinking I might buy that dress."

"That would be *amazing!*"

"It wouldn't be too much? It wouldn't be inappropriate for somebody my age, with my track record?"

"Um, no!" said Piper. "It's your day. Wear what you want to wear. And it's not bright, bright white. It's ivory."

"And that makes it less young and virginal?" asked Glenna.

"Totally," said Piper. "What about a bridal party?"

"Only Susannah and Arthur," said Glenna. "Although the way it's going between Casey and his brother, who knows if Arthur will even show up."

"Ah, family dynamics," observed Piper. "Always fun."

"It's amazing how ugly things can get when money is concerned," said Glenna. "Quent was in here a while ago, asking me what I thought of seeing if Walden's would provide diamond jewelry to glam up the dream sequence. I told him it was a great idea. But, when he asked me if I would want to call Arthur and make the request, I had to tell Quent he'd stand a better chance of getting a positive response if he himself called Arthur. It was embarrassing to acknowledge that I'm not exactly my future brother-in-law's favorite."

A thought flashed across Piper's mind. *Would Arthur Walden be upset enough about his brother's upcoming wedding to actually try to prevent it from happening? What if the target of the cyanide had really been Glenna?*

"Don't worry, Piper," said Glenna. "I already thought of it myself. And no, I don't think Arthur would be capable of that."

Piper looked at her friend with surprise. "What? You're a mind-reader now?"

"The expression on your face gave you away. You forget, I know how that mind of yours works."

"Maybe you should let the police know about the situation anyway?" asked Piper. "Just to be safe?"

"Yeah, right. And the police talk to Arthur about it? What kind of relationship do you think we all could ever have after that? I'm hoping that things between Casey and Arthur eventually work themselves out. If I make Arthur a suspect in a murder, I doubt there would be any chance of us ever coming together as a family." Glenna shook her head, dismissing the suggestion and moving on. "Keep going, Piper. Next question."

Fifteen minutes later, Piper knew that while Glenna preferred fudgy chocolate cake, Casey was a plain-vanilla kind of guy. Piper asked Glenna about the flowers she would be carrying and whether or not she wanted something Christmas-related included in the decoration. Still, Piper had no idea about what she was going to do. She wanted to make the cake special, but there was nothing so far that seemed unique to Glenna and Casey.

"I'm looking for something with some romance to it, something that would be symbolic to both of you," said Piper. "Tell me about the way Casey proposed."

"That *was* romantic," said Glenna, smiling as she remembered. "We went to the last show of the day at the Hayden Planetarium. I didn't think anything of it, because Casey is such an astronomy geek. I figured he just wanted to see the show. You actually feel as though you're sitting among the stars, Piper. It's incredibly beautiful and, honestly, powerful."

"I've got to go someday," said Piper.

"You really do. Anyway, when the show was over and everyone else had left, Casey told me to make a wish upon a star." Glenna closed her eyes for a moment before continuing. "Then he said that I would make *his* wish come true by marrying him. He said that it seemed fitting to ask me there, because I was his star."

"Ahhh," Piper said with satisfaction. "That's it. That's the essence of your wedding cake."

Piper was about to leave when Glenna got a call from security. Phillip Brooks was in the lobby.

"Send him up, I guess."

Hanging up, Glenna groaned and turned to Piper. "Don't go. Phillip is here and I really don't want to be alone with him."

"I don't understand," said Piper. "Why are you even letting him in?"

Glenna breathed a deep sigh. "He's still Susannah's father, Piper. What am I supposed to do?"

"Set boundaries," said Piper. "Tell him he just can't come here. It's totally inappropriate. You have to see him when he picks up Susannah and when he drops her off, but coming to your place of work should be off-limits."

"You're right," said Glenna. "Of course, you're right. But at least I feel safe here, with everyone around. Phillip might make a scene, but he's not going to physically hurt me."

Piper stopped to consider her friend's remark. She knew Phillip had a horrible temper, but Glenna had never mentioned anything about it getting physically abusive.

"Has Phillip ever hit you, Glenna?"

"Not really."

"Uh, what does that mean?"

"When we were married, he grabbed my arm a couple of times and pushed me around, but he never really struck me. He does scare me, though, sometimes. He can't control his jealousy. And since he heard I was remarrying, I can tell that it's eating away at him. He's like a time bomb."

There was a forceful knock on the door.

"Want me to answer it?" asked Piper, getting up.

"No. I'll get it."

Glenna twisted the knob and let Phillip enter. His frame was imposing, emphasized further by Glenna's diminutive stature. Piper watched as Glenna seemed to shrink back from him.

"Hello, Phillip," Glenna said, her tone cool. "What are you doing here?"

"I wanted to see how you were doing . . . like always." Phillip leaned down to give his former wife a kiss on the cheek. Glenna closed her eyes, girding herself to endure it.

Phillip acknowledged Piper with a nod. Then, he thrust out toward Glenna the bouquet of flowers he was carrying. "I know how upset you must be about Travis," he said. "I hope these will make you feel a little better."

"Thank you," said Glenna with no enthusiasm. She didn't reach out to take the flowers.

"I can go find a vase," Piper offered.

"No, Piper. Don't leave." Glenna put her hand up.

"What's that supposed to mean?" asked Phillip, clearly insulted. "You don't want to be left alone with me?"

"Can you blame me?"

Phillip's face reddened. "You know, Glenna, I don't know why I even try to be nice to you," he shouted. "You are spoiled, self-centered, and ungrateful and that pathetic excuse for a fiancé of yours doesn't have any idea what he's in for. How long do you think it will take for you to tire of him like you did of me and go catting around for a replacement?"

"I'm not even going to dignify that with an answer, Phillip," Glenna said softly. "Please go."

"I'll go when I'm good and ready, and not a minute before," he shouted again.

Glenna turned to Piper. "Call security, will you?"

Piper already had her hand on the phone. Phillip pulled the receiver away.

"This is none of your business," he snarled. "Stay out of it."

Piper stood her ground. "You heard Glenna. Back off, Phillip," she said.

As she looked directly into Phillip's eyes, Piper was fully aware that in terms of physical strength, she had little chance. He was intimidating. But there was something about the way he used his size to bully Glenna that didn't scare Piper. In fact, it disgusted her.

"Phillip, if I were you, I'd go," said Piper evenly. "I'd go now. These walls are like paper and, at this point, somebody has surely heard you yelling. It's a good bet security is already on the way."

"Screw you," Phillip said disdainfully.

"No thanks, tough guy," said Piper. Even as she said it, Piper knew she had made a mistake.

Phillip reached out, grabbed her arm, and squeezed. She tried to pull away, but he held on to her too tightly, his strong fingers pressing deep into her flesh. Piper felt tears come to her eyes.

Glenna was trying to pull Phillip away from Piper but making no progress when Roosevelt arrived. The security guard grabbed Phillip from behind, wrapping one arm around Phillip's neck while pulling his arm down and around his back. Roosevelt pushed sharply up on the arm, causing Phillip to holler in agony.

Phillip was escorted away, passing through the small crowd that had gathered at the sound of the commotion. His angry voice carried through the halls.

"You can't keep me out of here!"

Piper rubbed her upper arm. "Wow. He's out of his mind."

Glenna was distraught. "Oh, Piper. I'm so sorry. Are you all right?"

"Yeah, I'm fine. But I hope this doesn't bruise." She cracked a crooked smile. "My dream-sequence dress is sleeveless."

Glenna went to the little refrigerator. Taking out some ice, she wrapped the cubes in a face towel and placed it gingerly on Piper's upper arm. "Do you think Phillip could be angry enough to have killed Travis?" she asked.

"I'm wondering if he'd be angry enough to kill *you*, Glenna," said Piper.

"Well, *somebody's* angry." Glenna reached for her purse. "I got another letter." She took out an envelope wrapped in a Ziploc bag.

"I'm being careful this time," she said, extracting the letter from inside the envelope and holding it by the edges. She began to read aloud.

> *"You didn't drink the potion.*
> *Here's what I'll have to do:*
> *The wedding's still in motion*
> *But it cannot be for you.*
> *So call it off, don't doubt:*
> *The mighty Casey will strike out!"*

"This time, you have to go to the police, Glenna," said Piper urgently.

Glenna nodded in agreement. "I've already called them. Somebody is really desperate that my wedding doesn't happen."

Or worse, thought Piper.

Chapter 34

As she observed the actors rehearsing, Martha Killeen seethed. She had better things to do with her time than to spend her afternoon dragging herself all the way uptown only to find out that Quent Raynor wasn't ready for his shoot. The nerve of the guy.

When he called the morning after the auction, Quent barely even mentioned the awful events of the night before. He had been all about begging for the photo session today. He claimed he was desperate for her to fulfill her auction obligation right away. *A Little Rain Must Fall* only had a few days left in the New York studio. He wanted the photos as a print finale. He had big plans for them.

Martha had shuffled around her appointments to accommodate him. Now, though, Quent wanted his actresses dripping with diamonds. He didn't want the pictures taken until Friday, when the jewelry would be available.

It wasn't that she didn't understand. She did. Viewing the all-white set on which the dream sequence would be shot, she could visualize how the sparkling diamonds would add to the images. But what really steamed Martha was that Quent hadn't called to let her know he was canceling for today. She'd only learned when she arrived at the studio.

Basically, she was doing this shoot for free, since all the money went to the Metropolitan School, but didn't Quent think of the value of anyone else's time? She almost wanted to tell him that everything was off. But she didn't want to stir things up, creating more problems for herself. Martha already had enough of those.

The press was notorious for getting things wrong, and she didn't need the word to get out that she was a prima donna or dishonorable. If she told Quent that she wasn't going to do the shoot, he could put the word out she had reneged on her obligation. Quent could conveniently omit the fact that he had canceled without warning. It was insulting.

She had overextended herself financially and had made some disastrous business choices. Her home had three mortgages on it and she had lost so much money in the stock market that she doubted she could ever recapture her investments. Her most valuable remaining asset was her genius with photography. That was what could pull her out of the economic hole she had dug for herself. Her reputation was her treasure and the last thing Martha needed was any bad press.

Times were tough and she had to do what she had to do. She had accepted a wedding job. Not that it was just any wedding, though. Glenna Brooks was a celebrity. And that had made it more palatable to agree to Glenna's fiancé's request earlier in the day.

As a rule, Piper would have been paying attention to every movement and spoken line during each part of the rehearsal. Instead, as Piper waited for her scene to start, she kept watching Martha Killeen. Piper was fascinated by the way the photographer moved silently around the studio, checking out various vantage points with a handheld light meter.

Piper was hoping that she would end up in at least one of Killeen's photos. That would be "ah-mazing"— the greatest memento ever. Piper knew she would treasure that picture for the rest of her life.

The instruction came from the control room, announcing that everyone could take a break. Piper went back to her dressing room, retrieved the box of gingerbread men, and came back to pass them around. She edged her way closer to Martha Killeen.

"Would you like one, Martha?" Piper asked. "They're from my mother's bakery."

Martha looked in the box. "Adorable," she said. "I don't care for gingerbread, but I'll take one for my daughter."

"How old is she?" asked Piper.

"Ella is six. She's in first grade at the Metropolitan School for Girls."

"I know," said Piper.

Martha looked puzzled.

"I was at the auction with Glenna," Piper explained.

"That was a terrible night," said Martha.

"Totally."

Martha extended her hand. "You know my name, but I don't know yours."

"I'm Piper Donovan."

"Nice to meet you, Piper. What part do you play?"

"Mariah Lane. I used to have a recurring role. Then I died. Now, I'm back for a week. I'm just happy to have the work." Piper didn't want to sound like a loser, so she changed the subject back to Martha. "I know you get this all the time, but I really love your work," she said. "Me and everyone else in the universe."

"Thank you," said Martha. "Sometimes it doesn't feel like the universe is on my side lately. You've probably read all about my problems."

Piper nodded sheepishly.

"Almost everyone has," continued Martha, rolling her eyes.

Piper nodded sympathetically. "You're a great talent, Martha. Nobody can take that away from you."

Martha smiled. "Thanks, Piper. You have no idea how much I needed to hear that right now," she said. "And I hope I'll see you at Glenna's wedding."

"I'll be there," said Piper. "I'm making her wedding cake."

Piper went back to her dressing room, thrilled that she talked to Martha Killeen.

She actually seemed to like me.

Piper put down the cookie box, took out her Black-Berry, and began texting for Twitter and Facebook:

I'M IN HEAVEN !!!

BACK AT ALRMF !

MET PHOTOGRAPHY GOD MARTHA KILLEEN !

DREAMS DO COME TRUE.

Chapter 35

Jessie was keeping two ledgers. One was for the auction bids, and the other was for funds coming in for the Travis York Memorial Fund benefiting the Metropolitan School for Girls' drama department. She would have to share some of the auction proceeds with other departments of the school. But, due to her quick thinking immediately after Travis was poisoned, anything that came in to honor him went for her projects alone.

Even with being cut short, the auction had raised over a million dollars and Jessie hoped Travis's memorial fund would bring in even more. Already the morning mail had brought three U.S. Postal Service boxes full of envelopes from Travis York fans around the nation. There were checks in a wide range of amounts. Some were big and some were small, but all of them were accompanied by notes of gratitude and admiration of the pleasure Travis York had provided.

There was so much to do that Jessie was working on getting her fellow teachers to come in and help her during their free periods. The contents of each envelope had to be recorded, and letters of acknowledgment had to be sent out. An attorney was making sure that everything was done legally and within federal tax guidelines. Jessie was arranging to make it possible for donations to be made via credit card.

The magnitude of work involved in the last-minute memorial fund made the auction look like child's play. The auction had been well planned beforehand. Since the guests were mostly students' parents, the school already had their e-mail addresses. Just to be on the safe side, everyone had to provide their personal contact information if they wanted to be able to bid.

Many of the bills had been settled immediately, and the winning bidder took home his or her prize. But there were a good number of items, mostly professional services and gift certificates for restaurants or hotel stays, that hadn't been paid for yet. Chief among those was the Martha Killeen photography session, which went for $100,000.

As Jessie composed an e-mail reminder to send out to the outstanding debtors, she was determined to collect every last dime.

Chapter 36

An announcement was made. Detectives were coming to the *Little Rain* studio within the hour to question cast and crew members. They wanted to speak to anyone who had thoughts or speculation about why someone would want Travis York dead.

A rehearsal hall was set aside for the purpose of assembling the staff. While everyone was waiting for the investigators to arrive, Quent Raynor strode to the front of the room.

"Before the police get here, let's go over a couple of unrelated things," Quent announced. "In case it hasn't spread through the grapevine yet, the reason we're postponing shooting the dream sequence is that I've arranged for Walden's Jewelers to lend us some of the store's most precious diamonds for our actresses to wear. That will give the dream scenes some major bling and should pump the Martha Killeen photo session as well."

"So when *are* we shooting?" called out a cameraman.

"Friday," answered Quent. "And don't get any ideas, anyone. Armed security guards will be accompanying the diamonds."

The staff twittered with polite laughter.

"And, on a much more serious note," Quent continued, "and just to reiterate, there will be no shooting at all tomorrow so everyone will be able to attend the service for Travis at St. Patrick's Cathedral at eleven A.M. A huge turnout is expected and security will be heavy, so I suggest you arrive early. Afterward, there will be a repast at the Sea Grill for our cast and crew."

Chapter 37

The N train out to Queens was packed with riders commuting home from Manhattan. Peggy stood, bundled in her navy wool coat, hanging on to a stainless-steel pole in the middle of the subway car for support. She stared out the window. The view was mostly of nothing, just the darkness of the tunnel interspersed with light at the various station stops.

As she rocked gently with the swaying train, Peggy's mind wouldn't stop spinning. First she thought about the costumes, mentally matching each one to the actor who would be wearing it. The schedule was so tight now, there was no time for mistakes or omissions. Every hem had to be stitched, every wrinkle had to be smoothed. Peggy hadn't left the wardrobe department all day, and still there was more to do.

Peggy couldn't think of anything she had forgotten, but resolved to arrive at the studio earlier than anyone else for the rest of the week. If something came up, she would be there to take care of it.

The train came to a screeching stop at the Queensboro Plaza station. People surged toward the sliding doors. Peggy slipped into a vacated seat.

It had been good to see Piper today. Peggy had missed her. But it bothered her that Glenna's nasty ex-husband had hurt her. Piper had shown Peggy the emerging bruise on her arm before she left for the day. Peggy reminded herself that a man like that really needed her prayers.

Looking down, Peggy caught sight of a white hair on the sleeve of her coat. She plucked it off, thinking about the police detective who had interviewed her just before she left the studio for the day. He had been very interested when she told him that she had briefly been at the Metropolitan School for Girls, shortly before Travis was poisoned. She had been long gone before the police arrived that night, and so had never been questioned before.

"Did you see anyone or anything that you thought was strange or suspicious?" the detective asked.

"No, not really," Peggy answered. "I was in and out of the building so quickly. I just ran in with the dress for Glenna, quickly helped her change, and then I ran right back out again. I had a cab waiting. It had already driven me from Queens to the studio and then to the school. It still had to take me back to Queens again. Even though Glenna was going to pay for it, I just wanted to hurry so the fare wouldn't be any higher than it had to be."

"All right, Ms. Gould," said the detective, handing Peggy his card. "But, please, keep thinking. Anything you remember might help. Sometimes, we don't even realize what we've seen until later."

Chapter 38

Piper sat on her bed with legs akimbo, sketching on a pad of paper. She had drawn two versions of the wedding cake. One with square tiers, the other with round ones. Even though she knew the square-shaped cakes were more contemporary and popular for New York weddings right now, Piper was leaning toward the round tiers for Glenna and Casey's cake. Round was more traditional. It went with the fabulous old mansion where the wedding was taking place.

Having borrowed her mother's recipe file, Piper calculated the size and number of tiers needed to serve one hundred people. There were various combinations that could work, but Piper had set her limit at three tiers. This was her first cake and she didn't want to be overly ambitious. A combination of six-inch, ten-inch, and fourteen-inch rounds would be enough.

She had decided not to use pillars to separate the tiers. Instead, she would stack them directly on top of one another. But even stacking required exacting measurement and dowels carefully cut and inserted within the tiers, distributing weight and making sure the cake didn't collapse into itself.

Glancing at the clock radio on her nightstand, Piper bolted off the bed. It was almost eight thirty, and her mother would be going to bed soon because she had to get up early in the morning to go to the bakery. Piper wanted to catch her before she went to sleep.

The door stuck as she pulled at the knob, the jamb still sticky from her father's recent paint job. The round knob fell off in her hand. As she tried to reattach it, Piper laughed in spite of her momentary frustration. The doorknob had been coming loose since she was a kid.

"Mom," she called as she finally extricated herself and hurried down the short flight of steps that led to the living room, dining room, and kitchen.

Her mother was standing with her back to Piper at the counter next to the sink. Piper saw her mother was putting a rubber band around a small container of chili powder.

"Why are you doing that?" asked Piper.

"I grabbed the chili powder instead of the cinnamon this morning when I was making French toast for your father," answered Terri.

"Good one, Mom. That must have been fun for Dad to bite into. I bet he loved that."

"Actually, your father was a good sport about it," said Terri. "He knew it was an easy mistake to make. The cans are the same size and same color. I'm putting a band around the chili so I'll be able to distinguish between the two."

"Reading the label also works, Mom."

Terri ignored her daughter's remark, placed the can of spice on the shelf, and closed the cabinet door.

"I've been working on the wedding cake," said Piper. "Want to see the plan?"

"Of course." Terri took the paper from Piper and sat at the kitchen table. She glanced at the sketches quickly. *Too quickly*, thought Piper.

"What flavor is the cake going to be?" asked Terri.

"Glenna likes chocolate and Casey likes vanilla, so I was thinking of marble."

"And icing?"

"I'm not sure," said Piper. "What do you think? Buttercream or fondant?"

"Buttercream is simplest and quickest and it can look wonderful, but if you decide on fondant, I can help you. You haven't done fondant in a long time and it takes quite a bit of practice to achieve that really smooth finish," said Terri. "What color are you thinking?"

"White," said Piper. "I think that will go best with the gold stars I'm envisioning. How do you think we could make big stars like those?" Piper nodded toward the sketches.

"Out of icing, with piping tips?" suggested Terri.

"No, I was thinking more of flat stars, almost like thin cookies that would be affixed to the sides of the tiers—or maybe even attached to wires so they look like shooting stars."

Terri considered the question. "We could roll out sheets of fondant and stamp out five-point stars with a cookie cutter," said Terri. "Then we could brush the stars with edible gold-luster dust. How does that sound?"

"Perfect," said Piper.

The wedding cake was supposed to symbolize prosperity, happiness, and longevity. Cutting the cake was one of the most cherished moments at any wedding reception. Piper wanted to make sure that moment would live up to Glenna's highest expectations. If the day was less than Glenna had imagined, the cake would not be the reason.

Piper went back upstairs, leaving the sketches of the wedding cake on the kitchen table. Terri picked up the paper and slipped it into her bag. She would take it with her to the bakery in the morning and slide it beneath the screen of the new vision-enhancing machine her husband had just installed in her tiny office at the back of the shop. Then she would really be able to see what Piper had planned.

Tonight, she had been faking it.

Sleep wouldn't come.

Piper lay in bed, first on her back, then on her side, finally on her stomach. She couldn't turn her mind off. The episode in Glenna's dressing room with Phillip Brooks kept replaying itself in her mind. She also had a physical reminder. Her left arm was sore where he had grabbed it.

She hadn't mentioned it to her parents. Why worry them? Besides, who knew what her father would do if she told him? Piper just wanted to ignore it and keep on going.

Ignore it, but not forget it.

Phillip Brooks was jealous and he could be dangerous. He was also obsessed with Glenna. Piper wondered if Phillip would actually be angry enough to punish Travis York for his relationship with Glenna when Phillip was away in prison.

These kinds of thoughts are not going to help me fall asleep.

She switched her focus to the wedding cake. If she did say so herself, her ideas were really quite good. She wished her mother had taken a better look at the sketches. It didn't make sense. Since Piper was small, her mother paid attention to every drawing that Piper brought home. Why now, especially when it was drawings of a subject she loved, had her mother barely glanced at Piper's work?

Something was wrong.

Piper's face grew hot as she began to put together what she had observed. Her mother had been knocking things over, mixing up labels and ingredients when she cooked, and, most of all, she had been avoiding looking Piper in the eye. Though she usually insisted on operating the video camera herself, she had turned it over to Piper for the bakery commercial. And, come to think of it, she hadn't seen her mother pick up a piping bag lately. Cathy had been doing the cake-decorating every time Piper had come into the bakery.

Springing out of bed, Piper turned on the lamp and went to her computer. After searching around and reading for fifteen minutes, she was almost certain her mother had macular degeneration.

Her mother wasn't saying no to the wedding cakes because she was too busy. She was saying no because she couldn't see.

Chapter 39

Tuesday, December 14 . . .
Ten days until the wedding

Fifth Avenue traffic was jammed, caused by the combination of motorists slowing to get a glimpse of the Rockefeller Center Christmas tree and rubber-necking to see who was arriving on the sidewalk in front of St. Patrick's Cathedral to attend Travis York's funeral. Uniformed police officers were stationed in the middle of the street, blowing their whistles and urgently waving drivers to keep it moving. Pedestrians crowded crosswalks. Car horns blared intermittently, adding to the tension.

Certain that traffic near the cathedral would be a mess, Piper parked the car in a garage eight blocks away. As she walked with long strides toward the church, she calculated how much it was going to cost to get the car back. She estimated $40 to $50, which she really couldn't afford to spend. She should have gotten up super-early and taken the train into the city. That had been her plan, but when her alarm sounded while it was still pitch-dark outside, Piper had rolled over.

Going back to sleep was something she would never do on a morning when she knew she had to get to the set for a taping or a rehearsal. Those she was eager to attend; the service for Travis was something she dreaded.

Police barricades had been set up to keep spectators and press back from the VIPs getting out of limousines and yellow taxis. Camera crews jockeyed for the best positions, eager to capture images that the producers of their respective shows would prize. They elbowed their way forward when they spotted a celebrity.

Piper squeezed her way through the crowds on the sidewalk, edging closer to the magnificent, neo-Gothic-style cathedral. She could see that lines had formed in front of each of the side entrances flanking the massive main bronze doors, cast with images of American saints. She suspected that the backup at the side doors had to do with security checks inside.

Finding the end of the line, Piper settled in for a long wait, but things moved along steadily. She soon progressed from the sidewalk to the cathedral steps. From the slightly elevated position, Piper could better see who was waiting behind her. She recognized Arthur Walden. And several people behind him, was Phillip Brooks. Piper hadn't expected to see Phillip paying his respects to a man he had so clearly resented.

Near the top of the steps, the woman in front of Piper turned around. Her face was somewhat familiar.

"I've never seen anything like this before," the woman said, shaking her head. "It's something, isn't it?"

"Amazing," answered Piper.

"I wonder what Travis York would say if he could see." The woman gestured expansively with her gloved hand. "It's quite a tribute."

"Did you know Travis?" asked Piper.

"Not really," said the woman. "I only met him on the night he died. But I'll be forever grateful to him for the way he helped our school financially. Not just that night at the auction, but the donations have been flowing in in his honor since."

"Oh? Do you have a child who is a student at the Metropolitan?" asked Piper.

"No, I'm a teacher there, head of the drama department." The woman took off her glove and held out her hand. "I'm Jessie Terhune."

Piper realized she was talking with the woman who had been involved with Casey Walden before he met Glenna.

"I'm Piper Donovan," she said, shaking hands.

"And how did you know Travis?"

"I used to work with him on *A Little Rain Must Fall*."

"You're an actress?"

"Yes," said Piper.

Immediately, Piper sensed that Jessie was assessing the information, knowing that if Piper had worked on *A Little Rain Must Fall*, it stood to reason that Piper would also know Glenna Brooks. Piper was prepared to say only the most glowing things about her friend in response to any comment Jessie might make, but Jessie didn't pursue the conversation. She just nodded and turned around again.

Chapter 40

When she saw the security guards flagging people with knapsacks, large purses, and briefcases off the line, Martha was glad she had decided against bringing her camera gear. She only had a small, flat pouch slung over her shoulder. When she arrived at the long table that had been set up just inside the church doors to serve as a search station, the guard nodded and waved her on.

As she slowly walked up the long aisle through the nave of the cathedral, Martha's head turned from side to side. Her photographer's eye was bombarded with images of people who heroically devoted themselves to God. Now their accomplishments were celebrated in stained-glass windows, statues, and side altars.

There were colorful interpretations of Elizabeth, Queen of Hungary, bearing a basket of roses transformed from bread for the poor; St. John the Evangelist holding a chalice from which sprang a serpent; the archangel Gabriel announcing to the Virgin Mary that she would be the Mother of God; and dozens of other religious stories artfully depicted in glass. A shrine to Elizabeth Ann Seton, the first American-born saint—which featured panels including scenes of New York Harbor, since she had lived in New York City, and Emmitsburg, Maryland, where she founded the Sisters of Charity— was one among many that graced the walls. Martha's favorite was the Altar of the Holy Face, where a mosaic image of Christ's face on Veronica's veil shone from the back wall.

She took a seat in the pew perpendicular to that altar and noticed that Christ's eyes could appear opened or closed, depending on how she positioned herself. Could he really see into her heart and know how relieved she was?

The money the newspaper had paid her for Travis's photos did not resolve her financial situation but had ameliorated it somewhat. It was wrong to be secretly happy when another person's misfortune led to your own bonanza, but it was human, too.

Chapter 41

Heads turned as another limousine pulled up at the curb. Glenna Brooks alighted from the car, and the camera crews and photographers sprang into action. By the time her fiancé came around and joined her from the other side of the car, the paparazzi were jostling for advantage.

Glenna braced herself for the usual barrage of demands, but the cameramen were subdued, quietly calling out "Glenna" or "Ms. Brooks" to get her to turn her head.

Glenna and Casey made their way up the steps as a black hearse pulled to a stop in front of the bronze-door entrance. Men in black overcoats unloaded the casket, and bagpipers, dressed in plaid kilts, black berets, and spats, stood on the steps, welcoming the body of Travis York into the cathedral.

Chapter 42

The priest stood at the foot of the steps leading up to the sanctuary, placing a teaspoon of incense over the hot coals. After a deep bow, he looked up to the crucifix while clanging the brass thurible three times against its chain. Following another bow, he slowly climbed the steps and walked around the altar, sending plumes of perfumed smoke into the air with each gentle swing.

Quent wasn't paying attention to the religious aspects of what was happening in front of him. He squirmed in the pew, eager for the whole thing to be over. The incense was bothering his eyes, and beads of perspiration peppered his brow as he thought about all the things he had to do and how the funeral was cutting into his precious time.

There were the final scenes to shoot, the huge move to L.A. to contend with, and, right now, most urgent on his list was talking with the *ALRMF* press agent and making sure he was milking the tragedy for all the media attention it was worth. The overnights showed that ratings had skyrocketed. Quent wanted to keep the momentum going for as long as possible.

Access Hollywood and *Inside Edition* had led with Travis's death on Friday night and with the investigation last night. Quent thought it was a good bet that the entertainment shows would start off with the funeral tonight.

Audiences were fascinated by murder.

Chapter 43

*T*he casket was positioned just in front of a central bronze gate decorated with kneeling angels, which divided the marble communion rail. In the sanctuary, on the other side of the saint-bedecked rail, steps draped with an antique Oriental carpet led to a white marble altar surrounded with banks of red poinsettias and six tall, shining candlesticks. On a massive column to the left, an imposing Saint Patrick stood guard over his cathedral, holding a sprig of shamrock.

At the deep end of the sanctuary, behind the front altar, was another, grander one, crowned with an intricate bronze baldachin full of symbolic decorations and figures of even more saints. The archbishops of New York were buried under the high altar, their *wide-brimmed galeros with hanging tassels eerily suspended from the ceiling high above.*

The red leather-padded kneelers were still a little hard on the knees, but it seemed an especially appropriate time to give thanks. The worst was over. The deed was done. There had been no negative repercussions. And, so far, it didn't appear that the police had a clue who had killed Travis York.

Glory to God in the highest.

Chapter 44

She tried not to look at the casket, tried not to think about Travis lying, cold and still, inside. As the priest blessed the casket with holy water, tears filled Peggy Gould's eyes. Her faith was being tested.

As she ran her fingers through her short, white hair, Peggy knew that it wasn't God who had poisoned Travis. It was a human being, with free will, who had taken his life. Yet she couldn't understand why God allowed something like this to happen. It was so senseless and such a waste.

She took some consolation as she looked around. The turnout for Travis's funeral would have made him proud. The pews were filled and people stood in the side aisles. Among the many Peggy didn't recognize at all, there were some that she did. Including the person she should probably tell the police about.

She *had* remembered something.

Throughout the remainder of the service, Peggy wrestled mentally. What was the right thing to do? What if what she had seen as she rushed past the school ballroom on her way to deliver the clean dress to Glenna had no significance? What if she told the police about it and an innocent person became the chief suspect in a murder case? There would be headlines and media scrutiny and, even if it turned out there was nothing to what Peggy had seen, the suspect's life would never be the same.

Thou shalt not bear false witness.

Peggy didn't want to be responsible for ruining somebody's life with a baseless accusation. On the other hand, she didn't want a killer to go free.

Chapter 45

The priest climbed the curved staircase that led to the octagon-shaped pulpit. Piper tried to make out which saints were carved on the marble sides, but she wasn't close enough to see. It didn't really matter. Unless their names were incised beneath, she doubted she'd be able to recognize them anyway.

Dressed in white vestments, the priest began his eulogy.

"Travis York was known to millions. And loved by them, too."

Looking down at her lap, Piper fiddled with the fingers of her leather gloves. She remembered the first time she and Travis had had a scene together. She had been so nervous. Yet he had put her at ease almost instantly with his self-deprecating sense of humor.

"He had a boyish charm and a ready smile, both on and off the screen."

What a loss of a good human being. What a waste of talent. What an outrage that someone would actually kill Travis York.

"But we are here this morning not just to remember what Travis said and did, but what the Lord said and did—for Travis, and for us."

For Piper, God's plan was hard to see in this. She wanted to hear the priest quote chapter and verse: "Vengeance is mine, saith the Lord." And if God didn't want to do it directly, Piper wanted the NYPD or FBI or somebody to bring Travis York's killer to justice.

She wished she could help.

After the service was over, Piper stood in respect, remaining with the others in the church as the casket was rolled back down the main aisle. She knew that Travis was not going to be buried today. His body was being flown back to Scottsbluff, Nebraska, to be laid to rest in the town where he grew up.

While she waited, Piper spotted Peggy Gould on the other side of the church. Their eyes met, and Piper signaled that she would meet Peggy outside.

When they got together on the sidewalk, Piper could see that Peggy had been crying.

"Come on," said Piper, putting her arm around Peggy's shoulders. "Let's go over to the Sea Grill. We'll have something to eat and drink. That'll make us feel better."

"You go ahead. I'll meet you there in a little bit," said Peggy. "There's somebody I want to talk with first. Wish me luck."

"Why do you need luck?" asked Piper.

But Peggy didn't hear. She had already turned and was walking back up the church steps.

Chapter 46

More than a thousand white candles sheltered in amber-tinted glass cups twinkled throughout the cathedral. Candle stands were located at the entrances, at the many side altars, and in various other places, making it easy to find a candle to light as a way to remember a loved one or pray for a special intention. Phillip wanted to light one before he left.

He held back from the other mourners streaming down the main aisle on their way out of the building. Instead, Phillip went toward the left, stopping at the Altar of the Holy Face. He stared at the dark statue perched at the side of the altar. Behind the communion rail stood St. Jude, the patron saint of lost causes. Most of the candles in front of him were already lit.

Taking his wallet, Phillip pulled out a bill and stuffed it into the donation slot. He picked up a long, thin wooden stick from the front of the stand, lit it from the flame of an already-burning candle, and transferred the flame to an unlit votive in the middle of the bottom row. Then he stood before the statue and bowed his head.

Phillip knew that many desperate people made promises that if the saint helped when called upon, a note of thanks would be published in the newspaper. He had seen the listings in the personal ads. *Thank you, St. Jude* or *St. Jude, I thank you for your intercession in response to my prayers.* Each notice represented a prayer that had been answered.

While he was in prison, Phillip had scoffed at his cell-mate's repeated prayers to St. Jude. It hadn't helped the guy any, as far as Phillip could see. Phillip hadn't bothered to pray back then. He had to do his time and there would be no miraculous intervention. The federal prison system would see to that. Phillip had been resigned to his fate.

But now Phillip knew the true meaning of desperation. He was in despair at the thought that his Glenna was marrying someone else only ten days from now. As each day brought the wedding closer, Phillip was growing more hopeless. And full of rage.

Glenna was his and she shouldn't be with another man.

Things had spiraled downward and his feelings scared him. It had been a mistake to go to the studio yesterday and confront Glenna, but he hadn't been able to help it. He couldn't control himself.

When all other hope was gone, St. Jude was said to be the one to call upon, though his help often came at the very last moment. Phillip prayed that St. Jude would come to his aid before Glenna's Christmas Eve wedding.

But in case the whole St. Jude thing was a bunch of bull, Phillip was going to take action of his own.

Chapter 47

It took her breath away.

Every year, for as long as she could remember, Piper had come to see the Christmas tree at Rockefeller Center. Every time it left her breathless. Even though the tree made traffic a nightmare, it had the ability to turn crowded midtown Manhattan into a fantasy land.

Piper stood at the top of the promenade that led from Fifth Avenue down to the outdoor skating rink, the fountain, and the colossal golden statue of Prometheus. The fantastic Christmas tree presided over all of it. The promenade was lined by fine stores and featured gardens down the middle, providing greenery and benches for rest. At the sides of the gardens, angels made from white wire and little white lights faced each other. They held up their brass horns, heralding the season and the ninety-foot Norway spruce. Two dozen electricians had spent two weeks attaching thirty thousand colored lights to the branches of the most famous tree in America.

Beneath the limestone skyscrapers, there was an underground city. It was an imposing network of walkways that led to the subway and to every building in Rockefeller Center. The vast labyrinth was lined with stores and places to eat.

Piper spotted the heavy glass-and-metal doors in the middle of the Promenade. As she entered the building, she was met by a doorman.

"Hi, I'm going to the Sea Grill," she said.

"Of course," he said, nodding in the direction of the stairway that led down beneath the ground.

Chapter 48

Peggy climbed back up the steps so she could get a better view of the crowd. She searched the faces of the people gathered in front of the cathedral. Many had broken into clusters, discussing Travis and the service. Others were getting into cars, hailing cabs, and walking down the sidewalk, away from the church. She was starting to fear that the person she was looking for was already gone, when she spotted the figure waiting to cross Fiftieth Street.

With determination, Peggy descended to the sidewalk and edged her way through the throng. She caught up in front of Saks Fifth Avenue. Feeling Peggy's tap on the shoulder, her quarry turned around.

"Excuse me. I have something I want to talk with you about," Peggy said, sounding more decisive than she felt.

Peggy's declaration was met with a quizzical expression. "What is it?"

"It's about what happened at the auction the night that Travis was killed." She spoke loudly, to be heard over the din of traffic. Peggy looked for a reaction. All she perceived was curiosity.

"Yes?"

Maybe I'm wrong, thought Peggy. *If I had killed someone, I wouldn't be so calm if I was confronted about it.*

"I saw you on the stage by the podium with the pitcher of water that night."

"I can barely hear you. Is there somewhere around here we can talk?"

Peggy thought fast about how to answer that question. She felt safe standing on Fifth Avenue with scores of pedestrians hurrying by. Yet this was not a conversation to be shouted over honking horns and screeching police whistles. Though she was starting to have her doubts, Peggy wanted an explanation for what she had seen. As long as they went to a public spot to talk, she would be safe.

"I know a place," said Peggy, gesturing to Saks. "It's right inside."

They took the elevator up to the eighth floor. Charbonnel et Walker Chocolate Café was tucked between Ladies' Shoes and the Home and Gifts Department. Bathed in pale pink paint and lit by crystal chandeliers, the enchanted corner was dominated by a counter featuring a conveyor belt that transported plates of croissants, brownies, scones, muffins, and every imaginable truffle under glass domes. Dark and milk chocolate, strawberry, lemon, pink champagne, mint, cappuccino, and buzz fizz with its distinctive orange center. Sparkling glass cabinets temptingly displayed hundreds of the treats lined up in precise rows. They could be consumed on the premises or purchased to take away. A gold seal on the candy boxes signaled that the Queen of England was a fan.

"Let's sit over in the corner so we'll have some privacy," suggested Peggy.

As soon as they were settled, a waitress came over to take their order.

"I'll have a hot chocolate," said Peggy.

"Make that two."

"It's the most divine drinking chocolate that you've ever tasted," Peggy said nervously as the waitress walked away. Was she really gabbing about hot chocolate when she was about to discuss murder?

Chapter 49

One wall of the Sea Grill restaurant consisted of large plate-glass windows looking out at the skating rink. Skaters wearing colorful jackets and hats moved in a counterclockwise circle around the ice. Some held on to the railing for support. Some practiced exacting circles and spins. Most were just average skaters out for a couple of hours of fresh air and fun.

The cheerful apparel of the people on the ice, plus the multicolored flags of all the world's nations, which waved in the breeze above the rink, provided a welcome and uplifting view after the dimness of the cathedral. For the private reception, the tables had been rearranged, mostly pushed closer to the sides of the room, leaving space for people to stand and mingle in the middle. Waiters served wine and passed finger foods to the ravenous guests who were gradually arriving from the funeral service.

After checking her coat, Piper headed straight for the ladies' room. She found Glenna washing her hands at the trough sink.

"Glad that's over." Glenna sighed as she pushed the pump on the soap dispenser.

"Me, too," said Piper. "I think Travis would have been happy with his sendoff."

"Yeah, the priest did a good job," agreed Glenna, "especially for someone who didn't know Travis personally. Now *I* have to think of what I'm going to say for the toast."

"Isn't Quent doing that?" asked Piper.

"That was the plan," said Glenna. "But Quent's assistant just told me that he isn't going to be coming after all."

"Why?"

Glenna shrugged. "Apparently, he felt he had more important things to do." She rolled her eyes.

"Like what?"

"Something about talking to the press people. You know Quent. Nothing is more important than publicity and our ratings."

As she finished drying her hands, Piper changed the subject. "Is Casey here?"

"No. He had to get right back to school."

Chapter 50

T here's no point trying to deny it. You saw what you saw, Peggy."

"But why?" asked Peggy, her face contorted in incredulity. "Why would someone like you ever do something like that?"

"People do things they normally wouldn't when they're desperate. Believe me, I'm not proud of what I did."

Peggy observed the sagging shoulders, the down-turned mouth, the anguished facial expression. She felt a twinge of pity.

"Go to the police yourself," urged Peggy. "I don't want to have to tell them. It will go easier for you if you surrender."

"I have to get a good lawyer first."

"All right," said Peggy. "But you must do that right away."

"You have my word. I will."

Both were quiet as the waitress brought over the check and cleared away the hot-chocolate cups.

"You know, Peggy, I truly appreciate that you came to me before going to the police."

"I didn't want to be the one to ruin your life," said Peggy, "at least not without giving you a chance to explain yourself or turn yourself in."

"*You* didn't ruin my life. I did that all by myself."

They walked out of the café. Immediately in front of them were the attractive displays of the Home and Gifts Department. Baskets of painted hand-blown Christmas ornaments, tableware, perfume bottles, picture frames, vases, and all manner of house gifts were artfully arranged to tempt holiday buyers.

"You know what is bothering me the most right now?"

"What?" asked Peggy.

"My mother. She's going to be devastated when she learns what I've done. I can't even think about the Christmas she'll have. I guess, before I do anything else, I have to break the news to her."

Peggy nodded glumly. "I'm so sorry," she said softly.

"You've got to stop apologizing, Peggy. It's not your fault." They both stopped at a display of desk accessories. "Maybe I could get something here. You know, to have a Christmas gift for her when I go over and tell her. What do you think?"

"I guess so." Peggy shrugged. She thought of how shattered she would be if a child of hers had killed someone. She felt extremely sorry for the woman.

"Let me look at these. My mother loves anything with enamel."

They picked over the shelves displaying small clocks, boxes, and animal figurines.

"How about this?"

Peggy looked at the enameled letter-opener. It was certainly beautiful, long and smooth and encrusted with crystals on the handle.

"It's very pretty," she said. "Does your mother need something like that?"

"I doubt that anyone really needs a three-hundred-dollar letter-opener, but she'll think it's beautiful and, hopefully, that will bring her pleasure. She can use it to open my letters from prison."

Peggy smiled weakly at the attempted joke.

A blast of cold air hit them as they exited onto Forty-ninth Street. Peggy looked at her watch. There was probably still time to catch the end of the reception at the Sea Grill.

They walked together to the corner. Peggy held out her hand awkwardly. "All right then. Good luck. I'm trusting you to do what you said you would. Go to the police right away."

"You should be hearing about it on the news tomorrow. I'm sure the police will be eager to let the press know they have their killer. Thank you, Peggy, for letting me handle it this way."

"You're welcome and I'll pray for you," said Peggy as the light changed. She crossed over Fifth Avenue on foot, leaving her companion to hail a cab.

Peggy continued on Forty-ninth Street, telling herself she had handled all of this correctly. What was the worst that could happen? If the killer didn't go to the police immediately, she would.

I was right to offer a fellow human being the chance to do the right thing.

Still, something felt wrong.

Peggy jostled through the pedestrians walking hurriedly to their destinations. The elevator that led from the street level down to the Sea Grill was near the middle of the block. Peggy went into the glass-enclosed vestibule, pushed the button, and waited, watching out the window as a Zamboni systematically resurfaced the ice in the rink below. One of these days, she was going to get it together, rent some skates, and get out there herself.

Peggy was still facing the ice, wondering if she might still be able to do a spin, when she felt a gust of cold air. Someone had opened the door to the vestibule. She turned around.

"What are you doing here?" she asked, a quizzical expression on her face.

"There was something else we needed to settle."

Just then, the elevator doors slid open.

"Get in. I'll ride down with you."

Peggy's instincts told her not to get into the elevator, but she stepped inside anyway as the person she knew killed Travis York followed. It was only one quick floor down to the Sea Grill. What could happen in just a few seconds?

Before the doors closed, Peggy's hands sprang to her neck as the enameled letter-opener, in one swift thrust, was shoved into her jugular vein.

Chapter 51

After about an hour at the reception, Piper was ready to leave. She had spoken to just about everyone. The only person she hadn't had a chance to talk with was Peggy, but she was nowhere to be found. Perhaps Peggy had been so upset by the funeral that she had decided not to come to the reception after all.

Knowing that she would be seeing all the same people on the set the following morning, and conscious that by leaving now she could avoid the rush-hour traffic out to New Jersey, Piper headed to the coat check. While she waited for her coat to be retrieved, Piper took a couple of dollars out of her wallet for a tip.

She buttoned her coat and smiled at the receptionist as she walked past the front desk, on her way to the elevator. Before she pushed the button, the doors opened on their own. Piper stood back, waiting for someone to get out. No one did.

As she started to make her way into the elevator, Piper saw that there *was* someone inside. She immediately recognized the white hair and the navy wool coat.

"Peggy!" cried Piper, rushing to her friend.

Peggy was slumped against the wall of the elevator car. Her eyes were closed, there was blood all over her face, and something shiny was sticking out of her neck.

"Call 911. Get an ambulance!" Piper screamed to the receptionist, but the elevator door had already closed again. She grabbed hold of Peggy to support her. Piper tried to think of what to do. What had she learned in all those first-aid classes that her father had insisted she take?

Piper could hear Vin's voice. *Stay calm, assess the situation.*

It looked like a letter-opener protruding from Peggy's neck. Blood was dripping from the sides of the wound. The jugular vein. If that had been cut, or a carotid artery hit, it still didn't necessarily mean Peggy was going to die. If she got emergency treatment quickly enough, there was a chance she could make it.

But Piper wasn't trained and didn't have the equipment to suture the wound. Again, she thought of her father, suspecting he would have a suture kit in at least one of his various emergency-supply bags. She was never, ever going to roll her eyes at him again.

It took just seconds to go the one floor up to street level. The doors slid open. An older couple stood in the vestibule, waiting to go down. The pleasant expressions on their faces went slack as they saw what was inside the elevator.

"Please," Piper pleaded. "Call 911. Right away."

"We don't have a cell phone," the man sputtered as his wife clung to his arm and pulled him back.

Piper could see that she was going to have to let go of Peggy and get her BlackBerry out of her bag. She gingerly extricated herself, gently resting Peggy on the floor. Piper made the call, told the dispatcher the situation and where to come. While she kept the connection with the dispatcher open, Piper took off her coat and covered Peggy with it. They waited together for the EMTs to arrive.

Chapter 52

L ombardi?"

"Yeah, boss?"

"Come on up here. I want to talk to you."

Jack got up from his desk, walked across the squad room and up the stairs to the office of the special agent in charge. Jack already knew the conversation would be about the ongoing data the Bureau was collecting on terrorist funding. Knowing where the terrorists were getting their money was critical in the efforts to fight them. But the network of criminal organizations, money launderers, and illegal drug traffickers who were aiding the terrorists was vast and complicated. While progress was being made in shutting down some of it, there was still a long way to go.

As his boss started to brief him on the new information, Jack forced himself to concentrate. Something else had been on his mind for the past few days. He didn't like that he could have been wrong about the letter that Glenna Brooks had received. It bothered him even more that someone might have died because of his cavalier attitude.

Jack had been trying to remember the wording of the letter Piper had shown him. The only thing that struck a chord was the phrase from the old poem.

Casey at the bat.

Chapter 53

Piper took Peggy's limp wrist and felt for a pulse. When she finally detected it, it was rapid and very weak. Her breath was shallow and her skin was cool and clammy.

Piper knew the signs of shock. She also knew that shock could be fatal.

Concentrating as intensely as she could, Piper remembered that it was important to elevate the shock victim's legs, to make sure blood flowed to the organs and brain. She worried that by doing so she was going to make more blood flow to Peggy's neck wound. But Piper was scared. If Peggy didn't get blood to her brain, there could be neurological damage.

Piper stuffed her oversize bag under Peggy's feet, but it didn't seem to provide enough elevation. Piper took off her boots, folded them, and shoved them under the bag, gaining a few more inches.

"Peggy, Peggy," Piper said gently as she leaned over the wounded woman. "It's going to be all right. Help is on the way."

Peggy's eyes were wide open. Her pupils were dilated and she was staring into space.

Chapter 54

New Yorkers barely noticed an ambulance. While they might turn their heads at the sight of an emergency medical crew arriving at a scene of an accident, they didn't stop and gawk. They kept going.

But sightseers did pause to watch the skaters on the ice rink below. Leaning against the railing made it easy to blend in with them and possible to at least partially see what was going on in the glass bubble that housed the *Sea Grill* elevator.

Two medical technicians were bent over, attending to someone who was out of viewing range but certain to be Peggy. The techs were spending a lot of time in there trying to save her life.

Please, let them fail.

If there had been more time to plan, the attack would have been better thought-out, more certain in its outcome. As it was, the idea had seemed to make sense. On television, in the movies, and in suspense novels, a stab in the jugular vein inevitably proved fatal.

What if the movies and books were wrong? And what if someone rushing along the sidewalk had witnessed the stabbing? Of course, that was a possibility, but it was doubtful. Peggy had been trapped, her body blocked from view. The letter opener was thrust in a nanosecond, Peggy's eyes widening as the elevator doors slid shut.

There had been no other choice. The risk of Peggy telling anyone what she knew was too great. The chance had to be taken.

Eventually, the technicians rolled the stretcher out of the glass enclosure. The body was covered by a blanket, but not the pale face.

Peggy was still alive!

Chapter 55

It was dark outside when Piper left the hospital. She was exhausted and shaken. Though her parents' car was still in the parking garage, and it would cost a small fortune to leave it there, she didn't want to drive home, didn't want her parents to see her like this. She hailed a cab and told the driver to take her downtown.

As she sat in the backseat, she called her parents to fill them in on what had happened, before they heard about it on the news.

No answer.

Piper turned off her BlackBerry. There was really only one person she wanted to talk to right now.

The taxi let Piper off at the Twenty-third Street entrance to Peter Cooper Village. Built to accommodate returning World War II veterans and their young families, Peter Cooper Village was within easy walking distance to Gramercy Park, the Flatiron district, and Union Square. Over the years, the apartment complex, nestled in a landscaped park, had housed many FBI agents. The apartments were spacious and the rents were reasonable.

She walked slowly to the closest brick building. In the lobby, Piper pushed Jack's number on the intercom.

Please, let him be home.

"Who is it?" asked Jack's voice mixed with a little static.

"It's Piper."

"I'll buzz you in."

When she got off the elevator, Jack's apartment door was slightly ajar. Piper pushed it open.

"Jack?"

"Pipe?" The voice came from down the hall. "Come on in and make yourself comfortable. I'll be right there."

Piper stood in the small dining area just inside the front door. She didn't want to sit down, concerned that she might soil anything she touched. As she looked in the hall mirror and took in her disheveled appearance, she heard Jack's footsteps coming toward her.

"Hey! This is a surprise," said Jack as he entered. The smile on his face evaporated as soon as he saw she was covered in dried blood. "My God, Piper. What happened?"

"Oh, Jack," she whispered. "It was so horrible." For the first time since the ordeal began, Piper let herself cry as Jack held her in his arms and stroked her long blond hair.

Piper took a hot shower and changed into a pair of Jack's sweatpants and a long-sleeved Quantico T-shirt. Coming out of the bathroom with a towel wrapped around her hair, she walked to the living room and curled up on the sofa.

Jack came in carrying two plates. He handed one to Piper. Then he sat next to her.

"Mmm, scrambled eggs," said Piper, suddenly remembering how hungry she was. "One of my faves."

She took a mouthful and chewed, slowly and deliberately, the way she would eat if she had been ill but was now coming out of it. Her body craved food, but she was very, very tired. The events of the day and the long cry on Jack's shoulder were taking their toll.

"Ready to talk?" asked Jack.

Piper closed her eyes for a moment, images of blood and Peggy on the elevator floor coming to mind.

"It was terrible, Jack. But I don't want to go over it again, at least not now. I just want to focus on Peggy. She has to come through this."

"All right," said Jack. "But tell me exactly what her condition is."

Piper swallowed a bite of toast before answering. "They were able to perform surgery to repair the stab wound, but Peggy went into cardiac arrest on the operating table. They restored her heart rhythm, but they don't know how much damage was done. The doctors are also worried about neurological problems because of the lack of oxygen to her brain. So they gave her drugs to put her into a coma, to give her heart and her brain a chance to rest."

Jack raised an eyebrow. "I'm not gonna lie, Pipe. It doesn't sound good."

"I know," said Piper. "But at least she's still alive."

Piper opened her eyes. At first, she was unsure of where she was. The room was dark, but scattered lights from the buildings outside radiated through the picture window.

She was in Jack's apartment. She had fallen asleep on the couch. Jack had covered her with a blanket. Piper sat up and reached for the lamp. Switching it on, she looked at her watch. Two A.M.

She should go home. She had to be at the studio in six hours, no matter what had happened to Peggy. She couldn't go in wearing Jack's sweatpants. Or could she?

The main thing bothering her was that she hadn't reached her parents to let them know where she was. They would be worried. Piper was tempted to call them now but afraid to wake them up. She'd text them, but she knew from experience they didn't bother with texting. This was the problem with a grown woman living with her parents. If she were still in her apartment, they wouldn't know whether she had come home or not.

With determination, she threw off the blanket.

"Hey, watch out!"

Piper jumped. Then she saw that Jack had been sleeping on the floor beside the sofa. His hair was tousled and his eyes were squinting to adjust to the light.

"Oh, you scared me," said Piper, holding her hand to her chest.

"Sorry," said Jack. "What are you doing?"

"I'm going to catch a cab to the garage, get the car, and drive home."

"You've got to be kidding, Piper. Now?"

"My parents, Jack."

"That's ridiculous, you know that? Your parents aren't going to care."

"You don't know my parents," said Piper.

"That came out wrong. I meant they aren't going to care that you stayed in the city, especially when they hear what you went through with Peggy. They'll understand and be glad that you are all right. Just call them in the morning and explain."

Piper considered his words. Jack was absolutely right.

She lay back down on the sofa. "Wake me at seven," she said.

Chapter 56

Wednesday, December 15 . . .
Nine days until the wedding

C amera crews and reporters were waiting on the sidewalk in front of the *Little Rain* studio. For the second time in as many days, Piper made her way past the assembled media. One reporter asked for her reaction to the attack on yet another member of the soap opera staff. But none of the others bothered trying to question her. They were really waiting for Glenna Brooks.

The mood in the studio was subdued. People, for the most part, quietly went about their work. When they did talk about what had happened to Peggy, it was in muted tones and whispers. The only question on people's lips was: *Who in the world would want to kill her?*

Word had spread that Piper helped Peggy. Many people came up and thanked her. Quent Raynor was one of them.

"Piper, you don't know how grateful I am that you were there for Peggy," he said, putting his hand on her shoulder. "She means so much to all of us and when I think that she could have died . . ." His voice trailed off.

"Really, I only did what anyone would do," said Piper. "I just hope she'll be all right."

"Well, if she is," said Quent, "it's because of you."

Piper felt uncomfortable. "There were the EMTs and the doctors and nurses."

"Did Peggy say anything to you?" asked Quent anxiously. "Could she tell you who attacked her?"

"No," said Piper. "She didn't say a word."

Piper went to her dressing room and stripped out of Jack's clothes and her boots, noticing that Jack had missed a spot of blood when he wiped them clean. As she went to grab the terry-cloth robe she had left hanging on the back of the door, Piper caught a glimpse of the dark purple bruise on her upper arm, courtesy of Phillip Brooks.

Going to the closet, Piper saw that her dress for the dream sequence wasn't inside, and remembered that Peggy had insisted on taking it back to the wardrobe department to be steamed. That seemed so long ago now.

She realized that she must have been one of the last people Peggy talked to before she was attacked. That short conversation in front of St. Patrick's after the funeral hadn't seemed important at the time. Now Piper wondered if the person Peggy said she was going off to talk to was the person who stabbed her.

What did Peggy mean when she said "Wish me luck"? She must have felt she was facing something challenging, something that had the potential of going badly.

And Piper wondered about the real reason Quent hadn't come to the reception at the Sea Grill. Was it true that he was just too busy dealing with the press?

Not only did she need her makeup and hair done, she needed some serious camouflage for the nasty bruise on her arm. After an hour with the makeup artist and hairdresser, Piper felt she was worthy of trying on the dream-sequence dress again.

She went to the wardrobe room. Peggy's helper was there, looking drawn and frazzled. The room was in chaos, compared to the neat space it usually was. Peggy was exceedingly tidy and maintained a methodically organized department. In just the short time without her, the place was in disarray.

While Piper waited her turn for assistance, she walked over to Peggy's corner. On the small desk where Peggy kept her personal things, Piper saw the auction program Peggy had been studying on Monday.

Piper picked up the program and flipped through the pages. In addition to the listing of the auction items, there were photos of Travis, Glenna, the patrons who had donated, and the teachers who worked on the project.

Did Peggy see something in the program that sparked her memory?

Chapter 57

During a break in taping, Quent went to his office. As he walked into the reception area, his assistant was on the phone. She covered the mouthpiece with her hand.

"There's a woman named Jessie Terhune from the Metropolitan School for Girls on the line for you," she said softly.

"All right. I'll take it."

Quent went into his room and closed the door. Sitting at his cluttered desk, he took off his glasses before picking up the receiver.

"Hello, Miss Terhune. What can I do for you?"

"Actually, it's Ms."

"I stand corrected," said Quent, making an obscene hand gesture that Jessie wasn't able to see. "What can I help you with?"

"Is that what his name was? I forget. Ralph, what did he say his name was?"

Mr. Gould shrugged.

"Well, he must really value Peggy as an employee," said Mrs. Gould with pride. "He seemed very concerned."

"Peggy is very good at her job," said Piper. "Everyone loves her."

Mrs. Gould nodded. "I didn't know that Peggy had so many friends. It was nice that two others came by to visit and see how she was."

"Really? Who were they?" asked Piper. "Maybe I know them."

"One was a man and one was a woman," said Mrs. Gould, trying to recall. "What were their names again, Ralph?"

"I don't remember."

"I'm trying to get our auction accounts settled," said Jessie. "I'm calling to inquire about when we can expect your generous check."

"When do you need it by?" asked Quent.

"The sooner the better."

"You know, Martha Killeen hasn't done the photo shoot for me yet."

"Are you saying that you don't want to make the payment until she does?" asked Jessie.

"Well, I think I'd feel better that way, yes," said Quent.

"When will she be conducting the photography session?" asked Jessie.

"Friday."

"All right," agreed Jessie. "I could come over and pick the check up on Friday afternoon."

"Oh no, Ms. Terhune. I couldn't have you go to so much trouble. I'll send it over to you by messenger."

"It won't be any trouble at all, Mr. Raynor," said Jessie, wanting to make sure she had the check for $100,000 in her hands as soon as possible. "I'll be there Friday afternoon."

Chapter 58

After work, Piper went to the hospital. When she entered Peggy's room, she thought her heart would break. Peggy's elderly and frail parents sat beside their only child's bed. Their faces were etched with pain and worry.

Piper introduced herself. Neither of them seemed to recognize her name.

"How's she doing?" asked Piper as she walked closer to the hospital bed. Peggy looked like she was only resting, as if she could open her eyes at any minute. But her face was devoid of color.

"The doctor said to hope for the best, but that her condition is very, very serious," Mr. Gould answered glumly. "She's in God's hands."

"Did the doctor say how long they would keep her sedated?" asked Piper, deliberately avoiding the words "in a coma."

"Not exactly, but he thinks it could be a week or longer. He said that we didn't have to wait here, that we should go and they would call us if there was any change," said Mr. Gould, reaching over to take his wife's hand.

"I have a car," said Piper. "I could give you a ride."

"No, thank you, dear," said Mrs. Gould. "We have a lovely neighbor who is coming in later from Queens to take us back."

Piper nodded. "Well, can I bring you anything? I could go down to the cafeteria or run out to a deli and get you sandwiches or soup or something."

"That's very sweet of you," said Mrs. Gould. "But I couldn't eat a thing. What about you, Ralph?"

"Nothing for me, thanks."

Piper noticed a vase full of long-stemmed yellow roses sitting on top of the windowsill.

"Who sent Peggy the flowers?" she asked.

"Her boss brought them over a little while ago," said Mrs. Gould. "Wasn't that nice of him?"

"Quent Raynor was here?" asked Piper with surprise.

Chapter 59

B y the time Piper got home, her mother was already in bed. But her father pounced on her as soon as she came in the front door.

"I don't like what's going on, Piper," Vin said sternly.

"Hold on, Dad. I just walked in. Give me a minute, will you?" Piper put down the shopping bag containing her bloodstained clothes. "I don't understand why you seem so upset. I called you this morning and let you know what happened, why I didn't come home last night. You have to stop treating me like a child."

"It's not that you didn't come home, Piper, or that we called you a dozen times last night to check on you, and that that damned BlackBerry of yours was turned off. It's that you're in the middle of a very dangerous situation. What kind of place are you working at?" he demanded. "People are dropping like flies over there—first Travis York, and now that costume lady."

"Those *people* are friends of mine," said Piper. She felt tears coming. She couldn't take her father yelling at her now, on top of everything else that had happened.

Vin read the expression on his daughter's face and softened. "I'm sorry, lovey. It's just that I know too well what goes on in the world and I want you to be safe."

"I know you do," said Piper. "I can take care of myself. You taught me how to change a tire and jump a dead car battery. And you forced me to learn self-defense and first aid. In fact, I remembered some of it yesterday. The paramedics said that elevating Peggy's feet and keeping her warm helped save her life."

Vin nodded with satisfaction. "I wish you had let me teach you how to shoot," he said. "Any woman on her own should have a gun as long as she's trained to use it."

"No way," Piper said vehemently. "I'm not going to start carrying a gun. You know how I feel about them."

"That's a lot of liberal baloney," said Vin. "Guns, handled properly, can save your life."

"While taking someone else's," Piper retorted.

Vin knew from experience that he wasn't going to change his daughter's mind. "Well, let me check your pepper spray. And you have to promise me that you'll *always* carry it with you."

After taking a hot shower and eating two containers of blueberry yogurt, Piper took her laundry, along with the bag filled with her bloodstained clothing, down to the basement. Emmett followed along behind her and Piper was glad for the company.

"How's my little TV star doing, huh, Em?" asked Piper, picking the dog up in her arms and feeling the reassuring warmth of his body.

As she sorted through her clothes, Piper saw that her coat had taken the worst hit, but dried blood was also on the cuffs of her sweater and the front of her wool skirt. She'd take those to the dry cleaner and see if they could be saved.

Piper leaned her elbows on the edge of the washing machine and stared into the basin, transfixed by the water pouring down the sides. She felt overwhelmed with sadness. First Travis, now Peggy. On top of that, she had suspected for two days now that her mother was losing her sight.

She had been tempted to bring the subject up with her father, but he was already wound up enough about her being tangled up in the tragedies that were happening to others connected to the soap opera. She didn't want to risk upsetting him more.

She had to talk with her mother and ask her straight-out. It was not a conversation that should be had on the fly. When the time was right, Piper would ask, though she was hoping her mother would volunteer the information.

No.

Actually, Piper was hoping her suspicions were utterly wrong. That's why she wasn't broaching the subject. She didn't want to face it.

The thought of her mother being diminished in any way shook Piper deeply. Her mother was a constant, always there when her children and husband needed her, though entirely taken for granted most of the time. Her mother had always been strong and healthy. Piper rejected the idea that her mother was vulnerable. That wasn't the way it was supposed to be.

Why was it that it took something bad to happen before you realized how fortunate you were?

Piper lowered the lid of the washing machine, resolved that no matter what happened, she was going to be there for her mother, just as her mother had always been there for her.

Chapter 60

Thursday, December 16 . . .
Eight days until the wedding

*S*o far, sleep hadn't come at all. In only three hours,
it would be time to get up. It was going to be torture
to get through the day without rest.

It had been a night of tossing, turning, and thinking
about the visit to the hospital. Peggy was in very bad
shape. Her neck was bandaged, her face was ashen, her
hands lay motionless at her sides. Her body remained
perfectly still.

Peggy looked like death.

But she was alive. And the doctors and nurses at one
of the best hospitals in America were using every mea-
sure at their disposal to make sure she stayed that way.
If they succeeded and Peggy survived, she would be
able to identify her attacker.

It was tempting to think of a way to finish the job.

Yet it wasn't practical. There were too many people around, coming in and out of the room to check on the patient in an induced coma.

All one could do now was hope, pray, and just keep wishing that Peggy died.

Chapter 61

Friday, December 17 . . .
Seven days until the wedding

Two men in dark suits guarded the metal case containing the diamonds. Arthur Walden himself had accompanied them to the studio. He had the case carried directly to Glenna's dressing room.

Glenna greeted her future brother-in-law warmly, embracing him in an awkward hug. She hated that there was ongoing friction between her Casey and Arthur. Money caused fissures in too many families. Glenna heard Casey's side of the financial argument many times, and while she knew Casey had an entirely valid point, she also knew it must be difficult for Arthur to consider giving up total control of the business he had run unilaterally for so many years.

She wondered how two men from the same gene pool, raised in the same family, educated in the same schools, could seem so totally different. Casey was easygoing, generous, and, except for this conflict with his brother, not focused on money. His professional choices reflected that. No one got rich teaching at a private school.

Arthur, on the other hand, looked worried all the time. Admittedly, Glenna hadn't known Arthur for very long. In fact, she'd had dinner with Arthur and his wife only once and then seen them again at the auction. But the impression she got was of a withdrawn man consumed by his business interests.

She wanted both men to work things out between them, hopefully before the wedding.

"Thank you for doing this," said Glenna. "It's so good of you."

"My pleasure," said Arthur. "Where can we put this?" He gestured to the case.

"Right here on my dressing table," said Glenna, as she pushed some jars and a can of hair spray aside.

The guards set the case down.

"You can wait outside, guys," said Arthur. When the guards were out of the room, Arthur opened the case and began to unwrap one brilliant piece of jewelry after another.

"The neckline of the dress already sparkles, so I think a necklace would be too much," said Glenna, as she inspected the gems. "How about these?" She picked up a pair of drop earrings consisting of round, oval, and pear-shaped diamonds set in platinum.

"Wonderful choice," said Arthur. "These are exquisite. In total, there are over eleven carats. The color and clarity are superb. Together with your engagement ring, Walden's will be well represented and Quent should be satisfied that you glitter enough."

Glenna held the earrings up, watching them dangle as she looked in the mirror. "What do these sell for?" she asked.

"Retail? About five hundred thousand."

"I like them," said Glenna. "Who wouldn't?"

"You can wear them at the wedding, too, if you want," said Arthur.

"Really?" asked Glenna.

"Of course. They can be your 'something borrowed.'" Arthur smiled broadly.

"I really should put on the dress I'll be wearing with them, so we can see how they look."

"All right," said Arthur. "We'll wait outside in the hall."

As the door closed behind him, Glenna wondered if she had misjudged Arthur Walden. Maybe Arthur was a good guy after all.

Chapter 62

Piper was stretched out on the chaise longue in her dressing room, going over her lines, when her BlackBerry vibrated. It was Jack.

"I can't talk long," he said, "but I have good news and bad news."

"I'll take the good news first," said Piper as she put down the script, swung her legs to the floor, and sat up straight.

"They lifted a fingerprint from that second letter Glenna received—one that didn't match any of the prints she volunteered when she turned over the letter."

"Great!"

"But here's the bad news," said Jack. "The print wasn't in the system."

Piper's shoulders sagged. They were no closer to discovering who had sent the letters to Glenna.

"That eliminates Phillip Brooks," said Piper. "A convicted felon, served a prison sentence. His fingerprints would certainly be in the system."

"True," said Jack. "But just because he didn't send the letters to Glenna doesn't mean he didn't kill Travis or try to kill Peggy."

Piper considered Jack's reasoning. It *was* possible that the threatening letters, Travis's murder, and the attack on Peggy weren't related at all. Maybe the letter writer and the murderer *were* two different people.

Chapter 63

It had become a challenge for him. He was going to return and gain admittance to the studio. No matter what.

Phillip had been thinking about it since he was kicked out of the place on Monday. Going through the entrance where Roosevelt stood guard was a nonstarter. He'd never get past him. But there was more than one way to skin a cat.

There was a loading dock at the back of the building. Three giant garage-size openings were several feet off the ground, set up for truck cargo to be loaded and unloaded. There was also a standard-size door on street level. In the early years of their marriage, he and Glenna had used that door a few times when Glenna wanted to avoid press, who were camped out front for one reason or another.

Phillip knew that there was a guard's station inside the door. He had also observed that the guard sometimes left his post to take a break or talk with the truck drivers. He remembered thinking how easy it would be for someone to sneak past the unguarded station and keep on going.

The time to test his hypothesis had come.

Chapter 64

Piper had never really understood all the fuss about diamonds, but even she had to admit that the bracelet she wore on her arm was exquisite. It was an intricate geometric cuff with round, brilliant-cut diamonds set in platinum. She had no idea what it cost and, while she was curious, she made no effort to find out. She was concerned that if she knew how much the diamonds she was wearing were actually worth, she'd be worried and distracted. With the diamond bracelet sparkling elegantly on her wrist, she thought any more jewelry would be overkill and take away from the dress. But, to satisfy Quent, she had also selected sizable diamond clips for her ears.

Here she was, standing with the cast in a designer gown, her hair coiffed to perfection and her makeup absolutely flawless as Martha Killeen snapped away. It was all a bit surreal. Piper had fantasized about a scenario like this countless times, and here it was, happening. Of course, in Piper's fantasies, she was going home to a spectacular Tribeca loft, where the love of her life was eagerly anticipating her arrival. Oddly enough, she had never imagined that a moment like this would be coupled with a stalled career, living in her childhood bedroom . . . and murder.

If Quent got the Killeen pictures placed with the right magazines, chances were good that Gabe would get some calls. Industry people poured over pictures in *Vanity Fair*. Attention there, or in any magazine, would do nothing but help her.

When the time came to do her scenes, Piper was as happy as she'd ever been with one of her performances. While it was tempting to go over the top in her portrayal of a ghost, Piper deliberately played it straight. In the final scene, which she shot with Glenna, Piper was determined not to do anything that could be perceived as trying to wrest attention from the star. Not that Piper could, even if she tried.

"Nice job, ladies," Quent announced over the audio system after the scene was over. "And, Piper, maybe we'll have to figure out a way to bring Mariah Lane back to life so you can come out to Los Angeles with us."

Piper smiled. "I think that's a fantastic idea," she said.

Chapter 65

Roosevelt called up to Quent Raynor's office.

"There's a Ms. Terhune here to see Mr. Raynor," he said, looking at the stern-faced woman who stood in front of the security desk. She reminded him of his sour second-grade teacher, the one who had made him sit in the front of the room, displayed to all his classmates, after he wet his pants. The reason he hadn't gone to the boys' room was that he was afraid to ask her for permission. Roosevelt hadn't been able to make it to recess. He still cringed at the memory of the humiliation that dreadful woman had caused.

"I'll be right down to get her," said Quent's assistant. "She doesn't know her way around the building."

Roosevelt pointed to a group of barrel chairs arranged for viewing the television set mounted on the lobby wall.

"Mr. Raynor's assistant will be here in a moment," he said. "You can sit down if you want."

"No, thank you," Jessie said stiffly. "If the assistant is really coming in a moment, there's no sense in sitting, is there?"

Roosevelt was relieved when Ms. Terhune was escorted away. That was not a happy lady.

This was where she belonged.

Jessie liked the energy of this place. It was exciting to know that she was in the studio where professional actors, known to so many people, practiced their art.

If I had gotten the right chances, I could be here, too.

As she was being escorted through the halls, Jessie viewed the large black-and-white photos on the walls, showing characters and scenes from *A Little Rain Must Fall.* She noticed they hadn't taken Travis York's picture down.

"Will you be shipping all these pictures out to the West Coast?" Jessie asked.

"I think so," said the assistant.

"Well, if you are willing to sell the one of Travis York, I'd like to buy it," said Jessie. "It would be nice to hang it at our school to honor all he has done for us."

"I'll talk to Quent about it," said the assistant, as they reached the office. "Okay now, let me see where Quent left the envelope for you."

Jessie waited in the doorway as the assistant searched the top of the cluttered desk.

"I don't see it," said the assistant. "Quent's in the control room while they're taping. Wait here, and I'll see if I can ask him. It might take a few minutes. I don't *dare* interrupt him in the middle of a scene."

Five minutes stretched to ten. Jessie shifted from foot to foot. There was no place for her to sit. The sofa and every chair were covered with piles of books, files, and cardboard moving cartons. As Jessie finally sat on the arm of the sofa, her purse brushed against a pile, knocking papers all over the floor.

Jessie scrambled to collect the strewn documents. As she tried to gather them up, she realized there was no way to put them back in the same order. Her face flushed when she happened to notice the heading on one. It was an article on cyanide poisoning, printed from the Internet.

Chapter 66

"That's it, everybody. It's a wrap." Quent's voice boomed across the set. "But hang around, gang. Champagne and cake are coming."

Everyone applauded. Piper smiled brightly, but she felt tears welling in her eyes. She hated that it was over. But that was nothing in comparison to how upset she was about Travis and Peggy.

Piper was glad that she had fought back her tears when Martha Killeen came over and asked if she would like some individual shots taken.

"Um, yes. Yes, I would," Piper said in disbelief. She hesitated. "I don't think I could afford it, though."

"It's not going to cost you a thing," said Martha. "I'm here anyway and it'll make me feel good to do it."

"Wow, thank you so much!" said Piper. "That's very kind of you."

"Don't give it another thought," Martha said as she smiled. "Anyway, I want to hang around for some champagne."

Piper was listening to Martha's thoughts about how she wanted Piper to pose when she felt a tap on the shoulder.

Piper turned to see a looming security guard.

"I need that bracelet, miss, and those earrings," he said.

"Bummer," said Piper as she reached to take off the bracelet. "It would be great to be wearing this stuff for the pictures."

"You don't need diamonds," said Martha. "You're stunning without them."

Chapter 67

It wasn't difficult at all to hide amid the props, flats, and stacked cartons that were lined against the studio walls, out of camera view. Phillip kept out of sight and bided his time. As he waited, he was surprised that he felt nostalgic. This would be his last visit to the *Little Rain* set.

He heard Quent Raynor's announcement. Phillip slowly ventured out from his hiding place. He made his way to the edge of the set. He watched as stagehands pushed furniture out of the way so there would be an open space for people to gather.

"What are you doing here, Phillip?"

Startled, Phillip turned quickly. Glenna was standing there. His eyes swept over her, taking in every inch, assessing her, judging her. The woman standing before him in the beautiful white evening gown, with diamonds dangling from her ears, had to be with him. They were meant to be together.

"It was your last day. I wanted to celebrate with you," he said. "You look dynamite, babe."

Glenna momentarily closed her eyes and sighed. "Please, don't call me babe, Phillip."

"Once upon a time, you loved it when I called you babe." He reached for her hand.

Glenna pulled away. "Well, the fairy tale is long over. When are you going to get it, Phillip? I don't want to see you. I had you taken out of here on Monday and you have the gall to come back? Especially after what you did to Piper?"

"I didn't do anything to Piper," Phillip protested.

"Tell *her* that. She's got a black-and-blue mark on her arm the size of your fist."

"I'm sorry," said Phillip. "But Piper shouldn't have butted in. What happens between a man and his wife is nobody else's business."

Glenna's shoulders slumped in exasperation. "Number one: you always say you're sorry and that doesn't cut it anymore. Number two: we aren't 'man and wife' anymore. And number three: I'm marrying Casey and you better get used to it. In fact, I expect him here any moment."

"Admit it, Glenna. The reason you deserted me when I went to prison was that I would come out a financial wreck."

"That's it," said Glenna. "I'm not going to stand here and debate with you. Get out of here now, Phillip, or security will take you out again."

Chapter 68

When Quent's assistant returned to the office, Jessie was waiting. Nothing was amiss. All the papers had been restacked and were resting on the sofa.

"I'm sorry it took so long," said the assistant. "Quent has the check, but he says he wants to give it to you himself. He asks that you come and join him on the set and have a glass of champagne to celebrate our last day here."

"I don't drink," said Jessie, "but I'd love to go to the set, especially on such a special occasion."

"There he is," said the assistant, pointing across the room. "I'll bring you over to him."

Jessie looked ahead and saw Quent. He had his arm around Glenna Brooks's waist and he was laughing.

To her dismay, she saw Casey walk over and join them. There was no way she wanted to go over there right now.

"I don't want to interrupt him," said Jessie. "Would it be all right if I just waited until he's freed up?"

"Sure," said the assistant. "Can I bring you a piece of cake? It was made by Quent's own caterer."

"I can help myself," said Jessie. "I know you must want to talk with your friends. Go ahead, I'll be fine."

The assistant hesitated.

"Really," Jessie insisted. "I'll be fine."

Jessie helped herself to a slice of the sheet cake, passing the serving knife to the man in the dark suit who stood behind her in line. She wondered if he was an actor, but she didn't think so. He and another man who accompanied him were dressed in almost identical somber outfits.

Jessie picked up a fork and walked with her plate to a spot on the fringe of the room. From that vantage point, she got a view of the whole scene. It was all so glamorous, such a fabulous way to make a living, so different from the drab quality of her own life.

Jessie was slowly chewing her cake when she noticed a figure at the side of the room.

Chapter 69

*T*he security guards were helping themselves to cake. The metal case was unattended. Cast and crew were busy socializing. They wouldn't notice.

Now was the time. Now or never.

Open the case, grab whatever was on top, and that would be that. Over in seconds.

Take a deep breath and do it.

It all went according to plan until the accusing eyes of Jessie Terhune signaled she had seen it all.

It was a sickening realization.

Chapter 70

Suddenly, Jessie just wanted to collect the auction check and leave. She was trembling as Quent came over to her. He reached into his pocket and pulled out an envelope.

"Here it is," he said, handing the envelope to Jessie. "I think this is going to be the best hundred thousand I ever spent. Martha showed me some of the pictures in her digital camera. She got some great shots."

"Thank you," said Jessie, her voice quivering. "I'm going back to the school with this right now."

She couldn't get out of there fast enough.

Chapter 71

With the push of a tiny key, the message went out to her fans on Facebook and followers on Twitter:

END OF AN ERA: ALRMF'S FINAL DAY IN NYC.

BONUS: MARTHA KILLEEN TOOK PICTURES OF ME !!!

Piper looked up from her BlackBerry in time to see Jessie Terhune rushing away from Quent and out of the studio. She wondered what had happened.

Looking around the studio at all the people she had worked with, Piper felt her throat tighten. She loved these people, how hard they worked, how committed they were to putting on the best possible production. She wondered if she would ever see some of them again.

Travis should be here.

Peggy should be here.

That reminded Piper. She called the Goulds to check on Peggy's condition.

Their daughter remained in a coma.

Chapter 72

As Jessie entered the Metropolitan School for Girls, she passed the headmistress coming out. She looked exhausted.

"What a week this has been," said Mrs. Cox. "I'm so glad it's over."

"Me, too," said Jessie.

"I hate these short days," said Mrs. Cox as she buttoned the top of her coat and looked out at Fifth Avenue. "It gets dark so early."

"I know," said Jessie. "But worse than the dark is the cold."

Mrs. Cox nodded. "Why are you coming back here now?"

"Oh, I just picked up the auction check from Quent Raynor. I want to make an entry into the ledger and grab a bank deposit slip. I don't want to leave a hundred-thousand-dollar check lying around all weekend."

Jessie's footsteps echoed as she walked down the hall. She peeked in the gym as she walked past. The lights were still on but the space was empty. She supposed the security guard was checking the rooms upstairs. On Fridays, nobody else hung around later than was absolutely necessary.

She went to her office, took off her coat, and sat at the desk. Pulling the auction ledger out of the drawer, she found the notation for Quent Raynor's name and marked it PAID IN FULL. She leafed through the other pages. In just over a week, she had made amazing progress in collecting all the money owed.

As Jessie went to put the heavy ledger away, it slipped from her hands and fell loudly to the floor. *Take it easy,* she told herself.

Her hands trembled as she filled out the deposit slip. When she thought about what she had seen at the studio, she knew she should call the police. But Jessie was certain she wouldn't. The police would ask too many questions.

She had done things herself that she didn't want anyone to know about. The last thing she needed was to be placed under any scrutiny. It was better to keep quiet.

Chapter 73

*C*limbing up the marble steps and walking into the entry hall was like stepping into yesteryear, a more formal, gracious, and elegant time. What privileged surroundings. The girls who attended school here were so fortunate.

It was very quiet. That was good. The place was deserted.

Standing in a dark hall corner, listening intently, would be enough. A sound, any sound, would lead the way to Jessie Terhune.

Minutes passed. Still, no noise.

Waiting was not going to work. It was going to be necessary to search the building, slowly, carefully, quietly.

Suddenly, a loud thud reverberated in the hallway, indicating where the drama teacher was. The sound was like a homing signal, coming from the end of the corridor, just past the gym.

The open gymnasium door seemed like an invitation. A basketball, a pair of forgotten sneakers, and a child's jump rope lay on the floor.

A jump rope.

Why use something that could be traced to its owner when a school jump rope would work just as well?

Chapter 74

The school security guard found Casey Walden kneeling over the body of Jessie Terhune, feeling for a pulse at her wrist. Her face was terribly twisted, her tongue hanging slightly out of her mouth, her eyes bulging. There was a line of bluish discoloration around her throat, a jump rope circled loosely about her neck and shoulders.

Casey stood up, pulled his cell phone out of his pocket, and dialed 911.

"Nine one one. What is your emergency?"

"I want to report . . ." Casey hesitated. "A murder."

Chapter 75

Saturday, December 18 . . .
Six days until the wedding

Piper got up early, showered, dressed, and ran the vacuum cleaner around the living, dining, and family rooms. Emmett accompanied her, seeming deliberately to roll on the rug and leave a new deposit of hair in spots Piper had just cleaned.

"Emmett!" she cried in desperation. "You're driving me up the wall!"

The dog happily trotted away.

Piper was eager to get to the bakery. After she finished the less-than-perfect vacuuming job, she poured herself a glass of orange juice and turned on the small television set on the counter. Piper was filling the teapot with water when she heard the morning news anchorman's voice.

"In Manhattan, the second murder in eight days at the prestigious Metropolitan School for Girls. Melissa Maddox has the story."

Piper stopped what she was doing and stared in disbelief as the report began. An attractive reporter, bundled in a heavy jacket, hat, and gloves, was standing on Fifth Avenue in front of the school. Her breath was visible in the frigid air as she began to speak.

"Right, Don. Thirty-nine-year-old Jessie Terhune, a drama teacher at the school, was found dead on the floor of her office last night, an apparent victim of strangulation."

Oh my God, thought Piper as she watched the images of a covered body being carried out of the building appear on the screen. *That poor woman. I just saw her yesterday!*

"Police theorize that Terhune was working alone in the building when she was attacked. When EMTs arrived, Ms. Terhune was already dead."

A police spokesperson weighed in.

"There was no sign of a struggle. It looks like someone snuck up behind her and strangled her. There was a child's jump rope wrapped around her neck."

Clearly shaken, Michele Cox spoke next. "The police showed me the jump rope. It is the kind we have here in our gymnasium." The headmistress shook her head, visibly trying to hold back tears. "I must have been the last person to see her alive. We passed each other on the way in and out of school last night. I know she had just come back from picking up a check at the *Little Rain* studio. Obviously, everyone is devastated."

File video of Travis acting on *A Little Rain Must Fall* was followed by shots of the crowd gathered for his funeral.

"Just last week, Travis York, star of the popular daytime drama *A Little Rain Must Fall,* was poisoned as he acted as auctioneer at a school charity event organized by Ms. Terhune. Police are also looking for a link to the attack on the soap opera's wardrobe mistress, Peggy Gould, who was stabbed Tuesday after attending York's funeral at St. Patrick's Cathedral."

Melissa Maddox was back on camera again.

"And there's yet another strange twist, Don. Ms. Terhune's body was discovered by fellow teacher, Casey Walden, who is scheduled to marry actress Glenna Brooks on Christmas Eve. As you know, Glenna Brooks also stars in *A Little Rain Must Fall.* And just a few minutes ago, someone told me that Terhune and Walden were romantically linked at one time."

Are the police looking at Casey as a suspect? Piper wondered.

When the report concluded, Piper turned to put her dirty glass into the dishwasher. Her father was standing in the doorway. By the scowl on his face, she could tell he had seen the news report, too.

"Please, Dad. Don't start."

"Ah, baloney," Vin said with disgust. "You think this is a big game, Piper. You don't think any of this could ever threaten you."

"I do *not* think it's a game, Dad," Piper protested. "And I'm being careful."

"I know your idea of being careful," Vin said sarcastically. "For Pete's sake, Piper, you don't even take an umbrella when it's going to rain." He gestured to the kitchen chair. "Sit back down a minute. I want to talk to you."

Resigned, Piper did as she was told. Vin remained standing.

"There's obviously a madman out there who's not above killing seemingly innocent people, a murderer who doesn't seem to care about killing in front of witnesses. Someone like that would do anything—and that *someone* has something to do with your world, Piper. That puts *you* in danger, too."

"All right, Dad. All right. Enough. I get it."

After Vin finished his lecture and went down to the basement, Piper tried to reach Glenna. The call went straight to voice mail.

As she left for the bakery, Piper wondered if the wedding was even going to happen. If the police thought

Casey killed Jessie Terhune, that meant the wedding could be called off, or at least postponed. Piper didn't think Casey Walden was capable of killing anyone, but so many times you heard of friends and neighbors of murderers having no idea a killer had lived among them.

"Hi, Mom," said Piper as she hung her jacket on the coat rack in the back of the bakery.

"Hi, sweetie," Terri said cheerfully, offering her cheek to be kissed. "All ready to work?"

If her mother had heard the news about Jessie Terhune, she didn't mention it. Piper didn't bring it up, either.

As each day passed since she had figured out her mother's problem, Piper was more and more impressed by her. Piper knew that if she found out that her own eyesight was failing, she would go into an emotional tailspin. Yet her mother didn't seem down at all. Instead, she carried on each day, doing the best she could, betraying nothing to the customers that breezed in and out of the bakery.

Piper still hadn't brought up the subject of macular degeneration with her mother, wanting to let her reveal it in her own good time. Nor had Piper talked to her father about it, but she didn't know how much longer she could wait.

Piper gave her mother a big, long hug.

"What's that for?" asked Terri.

"That's for I love you."

"I love you, too," said Terri, as she felt a cupcake to see if it was cool enough. "Want to help me out with something, Piper?"

"Sure."

"Would you frost these for me? In the front window? The customers like to watch, you know."

For just a second, Piper was ready to decline the request. She really wanted to get started on the buttercream icing for the wedding cake. It could be made well in advance as long as it was stored properly. But her mother needed help. That was more important.

Every time she looked up, Piper saw someone else on the sidewalk outside, watching her through the window. She smiled and, in the break between cupcakes, gave little waves, laughing aloud when one boy stuck out his tongue, held his thumbs in his ears, and wiggled his fingers.

She sprinkled crushed peppermint candy on top of the cooled cupcakes and then generously piped buttercream frosting, laced with peppermint extract, on top. She had to concentrate on the first few, but soon she was thinking about Jessie Terhune's murder.

It seemed a valid assumption that Jessie's death was connected to Travis's murder and the attack on Peggy. *But how? Who would want Travis, Peggy, and Jessie dead?*

As she swirled the icing on the cupcakes, Piper went over in her mind everything she knew. Travis had been deliberately poisoned with cyanide. That had to have been planned in advance. Though the victim was Travis, it could very well have been Glenna. Either way, why would a murderer take the chance of killing in front of so many people?

What if Peggy had actually seen the killer? Was that the reason she had been stabbed?

Piper thought back to the brief conversation she and Peggy had had on the steps of the cathedral. Peggy had told Piper to wish her luck as she went off to talk to someone. An hour later, Peggy was bleeding in the elevator, a letter-opener in her neck. Had Peggy confronted Travis's murderer after the funeral? If so, the murderer probably hadn't expected it and had to come up with a weapon on the spur of the moment.

Why had Jessie Terhune been killed with a child's jump rope taken from the school gym?

Again, it appeared that the killer had improvised a murder weapon on the spot. So, it seemed to Piper that while the first murder was carefully planned, the other two attacks had been more spontaneous. Peggy's confronting the murderer might have been the reason she was attacked. But what had Jessie seen or done that would make someone want to kill her?

Piper recalled the wrap party at the studio. She had seen Jessie talking with Quent and then rushing out of the studio. Did Quent have something to do with Jessie's death? As she thought more about it, she realized that, in a twisted way, Quent had benefited from Travis's death. The ratings had gone through the roof. That would have been the case as well if Glenna had died.

Piper's heart rate increased as she remembered that Quent hadn't come to the reception at the Sea Grill after the funeral.

Chapter 76

Piper slid the tray of frosted cupcakes into the display case and then went to the back of the store to wash her hands. She took her phone from the pocket of her jacket. Jack and Glenna had called. She listened to Jack's message first.

"Hi, Pipe. I heard the news about another murder at the school so I called my contact at the P.D. When they went through the vic's purse, they found a copy of 'Casey at the Bat'—you know, the famous poem? They're thinking that this Jessie Terhune was the one who sent the letters to Glenna Brooks. Seems she went out with Glenna's fiancé at one time and she may have still had a thing for him and didn't want the wedding to happen. Pretty crazy. Anyway, they're taking the woman's fingerprints and seeing if they get a match to the print on the second letter. I'll keep you posted."

Piper thought of the night at the auction, when Glenna had pointed out Jessie and said she thought Jessie wasn't over Casey. Though Glenna may have been wary of Jessie, she wasn't about to accuse Jessie of actually being the letter writer. As far as Piper knew, Glenna had not voiced any concern she may have had about her to the police, either.

Even if Jessie had sent the disturbing letters, she hadn't strangled herself. Her murderer and Travis's murderer and Peggy's attacker were still out there.

Piper felt certain they were the same person.

When Piper called Glenna back, the tension in her voice was obvious.

"Oh, Piper, everything is a total mess. We just got back from the police station. They were asking Casey all sorts of questions about his relationship with Jessie and why he had been at the school that late. It was as if they were suggesting that Casey had killed her and called for help to throw everyone off the track."

"Well, why *was* Casey at the school, Glenna?"

"He had gone back to pick up exams he needed to correct." Glenna's voice lowered to a whisper. "I think they are looking at him as a suspect, Piper. Can you believe that?"

For several seconds, there were no words as Piper heard Glenna sniffling. When Glenna finally spoke again, her voice was stronger.

"It's all so absurd, Piper. But I have to believe it will be all right. I'm home now, but we're leaving in a little while to meet with an attorney."

Chapter 77

Sunday, December 19 . . .
Five days until the wedding

Vin set up the artificial tree while Emmet circled in excitement around the family room. Piper carried all the boxes of ornaments up from the basement. As happened every year, strings of lights had to be untangled, and exasperation ensued when a lone bulb went dead, causing all the others to go out as well. When the tree was finally erect and bedecked in sparkling white lights, Piper and her mother began to decorate while Vin turned to his football game.

"Other families listen to Christmas carols when they put up their trees," observed Piper. "We're treated to the sound track of the New York Giants."

One by one, the ornaments came out of the boxes, familiar but each somehow a pleasant surprise. Terri had saved just about every pipe-cleaner candy cane, painted popsicle-stick frame, or Styrofoam bell her children had ever made, and she insisted on hanging each one of them. There were also glass balls that had belonged to Piper's grandmother, as well as a Nativity scene that was set up beneath the tree every year. Piper remembered how she had cried when she had accidentally broken the head off the Baby Jesus when she was five years old. Her older brother had tortured her about it, proclaiming that she was surely going to hell. Piper hadn't been quite certain what hell was, but she was terrified nonetheless. Her father had glued the head back on, reassured Piper, and sent her brother to his room.

Inevitably, some of the small wire hooks that connected the ornaments to the branches were missing and needed to be replaced. Piper watched and said nothing as her mother struggled with threading the hooks into the loops at the tops of the ornaments. But when her mother kept missing the branches as she tried to hang the ornaments, Piper couldn't contain herself any longer.

"Mom, you've *got* to be straight with me. What is wrong with your eyes?"

Vin turned his attention away from the television screen. He and his wife exchanged looks.

"This is ridiculous, Terri," said Vin. "She's a big girl. Just tell her."

Terri took a deep breath. "I have macular degeneration, Piper."

Piper took the news calmly, astonishing her parents.

"Are you seeing a doctor?" Piper asked.

Terri nodded.

"What does he say?"

"*She* says there are a lot of new treatments. We're going to be figuring out which ones to try. In the meantime, I have vitamins and supplements to take and I have to pay more attention to the things I eat, like adding more dark greens to my diet. I've also started some visual rehabilitation."

"What does that mean?" asked Piper.

"I'm working with an occupational therapist who is showing me ways to adapt," said Terri.

"Like putting the rubber band around the chili bottle?" asked Piper.

"Exactly."

Piper summoned up her courage to ask the big question. "You're not going to go *totally* blind, are you, Mom?"

"No, sweetheart. That's highly unlikely."

Moving closer, Piper put her arms around her mother and held on to her. "I don't understand," said Piper. "Why didn't you tell me? Why make it such a big secret?"

"I didn't want you to worry, Piper, or feel any sense of responsibility that, now that you're living at home, you'd have to pick up the slack at the bakery. I'd never want you to give up acting to take care of me."

"I'm *not* going to give up acting, Mom. But, let's face it, there are lots of downtimes between parts. I'm going to help you all I can, because I want to, not because I have to. Decorating cakes is not exactly hard to take."

Chapter 78

Monday, December 20 . . .
Four days until the wedding

The last few days before Christmas were crucial to Walden's bottom line. Anxious to get to the shop, Arthur barely touched his breakfast. He arrived before any of his employees.

He went directly to the safe and opened it. Arthur took out the metal case that had been used to take the jewelry to *A Little Rain Must Fall* on Friday. He counted as he took out the blue velvet bags and cases. There was one missing.

A diamond necklace was not there.

Trying to keep his composure, Arthur started for the phone. As he picked up the receiver, the buzzer sounded, signaling someone was at the front entrance. When he got to the door, he saw his wife standing outside, and let her in.

"You rushed out so fast you forgot your medication," said Laura, holding out a prescription bottle. "I have some shopping to do on Madison Avenue anyway, so I thought I'd bring it over."

Arthur took her arm. "Come to the back with me," he said.

"What's wrong, Arthur? You don't look good."

"I'm not," answered Arthur, his face ashen. "I think the diamond necklace was stolen. Someone must have taken it while we were at the soap opera set on Friday."

"And you didn't notice until now?" asked Laura.

Arthur shook his head. "I just had the security guys put the case directly in the safe when they brought it back. All I can say is, thank God, we're insured. That necklace is worth seventy-five thousand dollars and we're in no shape to eat the cost of replacing it."

"The insurance premiums are paid up, aren't they?" asked Laura.

Arthur nodded. "Of course, I had to let go two of our salespeople to do it. But I wouldn't think of letting the insurance lapse."

Laura was quiet.

"What?" asked Arthur.

"You didn't take the necklace yourself, Arthur, did you?"

"What are you talking about?"

"For the insurance money."

"How can you even suggest that, Laura?"

"Because I know how worried you have been about finances," Laura answered, adding softly, "and desperate people do desperate things."

"I may be desperate, but I'm not a fool. If I got caught doing something like that I really *would* be ruined."

"Have you called the police yet?" asked Laura.

"I was about to do that when you came in."

"All right, I'll leave you to it," said Laura. She gave her husband a short kiss on the cheek. "I do love you, Arthur. Everything is going to work out."

"I hope so," he said.

Laura started to walk away, stopped, and turned around. "One more question," she said. "Was Casey at the soap-opera party by any chance?"

"Actually he was there for a little while with Glenna. Why do you ask?"

"Because the way you've been worried about dispersing funds to Casey, I wouldn't be all that surprised if you stole one of your own necklaces and then tried to blame it on your brother."

While he waited for the police to arrive, Arthur tried Quent Raynor's office.

"You're lucky you reached me," said Quent. "I'm trying to weed out what to take to L.A. and what to throw out. This place is a mess. Years of stuff that I just don't need. Oh, and thanks again for helping us out on Friday. I've looked at the tape and your jewels look fantastic."

"That's why I'm calling, Quent. I've just discovered that the diamond necklace is missing."

"Really? I'm sorry to hear that, Art."

"I put it in the case myself Friday afternoon," said Arthur. "And now it's gone."

"Uh-huh," muttered Quent, holding the phone to his ear as he continued weeding through a desk drawer.

"So, I think it disappeared at the wrap party."

Quent straightened. "You're kidding me."

"I'm afraid not," said Arthur.

"Let me get this straight," said Quent. "You're saying that, three days ago, somebody here stole your necklace and you are just finding out now?"

"It looks that way."

"No, Arthur," Quent yelled, pounding his fist on the desk. "I think it looks like you are trying to blame my people when you should be looking at your own security guards—who obviously were incompetent— or anybody else who had access to the necklace over the weekend."

"The only other person who had access is me," said Arthur.

"Then, buddy, I suggest you get ready for the police and insurance investigators to come a-calling and figure out what you're going to say to throw suspicion off *yourself.*"

"That's not helpful," said Arthur stiffly. "I was calling as a courtesy, to let you know what's happened. I'm sure the police will want to question you and your staff."

"Well, that's going to be a tough job," said Quent. "After we wrapped on Friday, some of the cast and crew were taking off for Christmas vacations, some were leaving for the West Coast. Good luck finding them."

Chapter 79

Tuesday, December 21 . . .
Three days until the wedding

Piper realized she hadn't done any Christmas shopping.

The thought didn't rattle her. She always waited till the last minute. But tomorrow she had to make the layer cakes, Thursday would be consumed with decorating the cake, and Christmas Eve would be taken up with Glenna and Casey's wedding. Plus, she and Jack had made plans to exchange gifts and have dinner tonight. So, today was the only day available.

She took out her BlackBerry and tweeted:

OFF TO POWER SHOP. PRAY FOR ME.

She always tried to do her Christmas shopping in Hillwood. There was something about the main street lined with trees strung with little white lights that felt much more like Christmas than the several giant shopping malls in easy driving distance. Piper also liked supporting the local merchants. She worried about the big stores putting the little ones out of business.

Her first stop was the bookstore. She selected a newly published volume on survival techniques for her father to add to his collection. For her mother, Piper chose a current book that was being compared to *Gone with the Wind*.

When she brought the books to the counter, Piper flipped through them as she waited for her turn with the cashier. She thought the print in her mother's book seemed small.

"Do you have this one in bigger print?" asked Piper, holding up the book.

"Yes, as a matter of fact, we do," said the cashier. "We have a whole large-print section in the back."

Piper scanned the shelves and found the book she was looking for, as well as a large-print biography of Vivien Leigh, her mother's favorite actress.

Next on the agenda was the lingerie shop that Piper knew carried practically nothing her mother would ever be caught dead wearing. She found a simple blue bathrobe and matching slippers for her mother and a nightgown for her sister-in-law. Piper was mightily tempted to buy the beautiful silk teddy on the mannequin for herself. But she practiced restraint. She was nearly at the bottom of her savings and it looked like the check she'd be getting from the work on *Little Rain* was going to have to last a long time. Anyway, the teddy would likely go on sale after Christmas.

Finally, Piper went to the men's store. They had the flannel-lined jeans her father liked. She picked up two pairs, along with suede gloves for her brother. Piper spent a good deal of time walking around, looking for something for Jack, ultimately deciding on a Prussian-blue cashmere sweater. It was also more than she could afford, but Piper bought it anyway. She'd worry about her credit card bill next month.

She did a lot of that.

Chapter 80

Jack had made the dinner reservation at Colicchio & Sons on Tenth Avenue. He was waiting at the bar when Piper arrived, carrying Jack's present in a shopping bag. She went to kiss him on the cheek, but as he leaned toward her, they ended up brushing lips.

"That was a nice surprise," Jack said, grinning.

They were promptly shown to their table. Jack scanned the wine list, avoiding the reds that cost more than a week's salary, and ordered the Gioveto from Tuscany.

"Whoa," said Piper, recognizing the name from her waitressing days at Sidecar. "We're really going all out tonight, aren't we?"

Jack shrugged. "Why not? It's Christmas after all and you only live once."

"That's the truth," said Piper. "Travis and Peggy and Jessie Terhune have made me realize it. Have you heard anything new, Jack?"

He told Piper about the theft of the necklace reported by Arthur Walden. "Walden maintains it was stolen at the ALRMF wrap party."

"There were a lot of people at that party," said Piper as she digested the information. "Do the police think the theft is related to the murders and the attack on Peggy?"

"It's a definite possibility," answered Jack. "They are also trying to track down where the letter-opener Peggy was stabbed with came from. Apparently, the handle was marked by the manufacturer and the brand is only sold in fine stores."

"Well, I guess that's something," said Piper. "But fine stores aren't scarce in Manhattan, or around the country for that matter. It could have come from any of them."

"Right," said Jack. "And even if you find where the letter opener was purchased, it doesn't mean you'll know who bought it because the killer could have paid cash. Unless something unusual stuck out with the salesperson, we're probably going to be out of luck."

The waiter came with the wine, presenting the bottle to Jack for his inspection, uncorking it and pouring a small amount in Jack's glass. Jack went through the expected motions, swirling the red liquid around, inhaling deeply, and then taking a sip. He nodded to the waiter.

"I was thinking," said Piper when the waiter finished pouring and walked away from the table. She told Jack about Quent Raynor not coming to the funeral reception, which meant that he could have had the opportunity to attack Peggy. And she mentioned that she had seen Jessie rushing away from him at the wrap party.

"Do you think Quent could possibly be the killer, Jack?" she asked.

"Anything is possible, Pipe," said Jack. "But think about it. Quent Raynor wasn't the only person who wasn't at the funeral reception. Anyone who wasn't at the Sea Grill could have attacked Peggy. And that leaves a pretty large field."

Piper took a sip of wine and considered what Jack had said. Who else would have a motive?

"Well, Phillip Brooks hated Travis York," said Piper. "And he's insanely jealous. Phillip can't be happy about Glenna remarrying. Plus, he needs money—so it's possible that he stole the necklace when he crashed the wrap party. What about him?"

Jack shook his head. "Again, Pipe. Jealousy and poverty are not enough to make an accusation of murder."

The waiter came back to take their orders. Piper wanted the winter salad with pumpkin vinaigrette followed by the lamb loin. Jack went for the butter-poached oysters and the roasted sirloin.

"When our food comes, let's not talk about this anymore," said Piper. "Let's just enjoy our dinner and forget all about this for a while."

"Fine with me," said Jack, sitting back in his chair and cracking his knuckles.

"What's wrong?" asked Piper.

"What do you mean?"

"There's something you're not telling me, isn't there?"

"What gives you that idea?"

"Because whenever you don't want to tell me something, you crack your knuckles."

"I'll have to avoid doing that from now on." Jack smiled. "I don't want to give myself away."

"Well?"

"You're not going to give up, are you?"

"Nope."

"Fine, Pipe, you win. If you have to know, that wedding cake you've been working on may not get eaten. The police are really looking at Casey for Jessie's murder and for the jewelry theft, too. Apparently, his brother told them something that didn't help Casey at all."

———————

After dinner, while nursing amaretto cordials, Jack pulled a small blue box tied with a red satin ribbon from his jacket pocket and placed it on the table in front of Piper.

"Oooh, Tiffany's. I'm excited," Piper exclaimed as she reached down and extricated Jack's gift from the bag beside her.

"You first," said Jack, with a twinkle in his eye.

"You don't have to talk me into it," said Piper as she pulled at the ribbon. "Oh, these are beautiful!" Piper held the pearl earrings up to her ears. "I love them, Jack. Thank you so, so much."

Jack beamed.

"Now you," said Piper.

In three seconds, he had the box opened.

"What a great color, Pipe," he said as his hands caressed the soft blue cashmere. "I thought you were saving your pennies these days."

Piper smiled. "Not when it comes to you, Jack."

Chapter 81

Wednesday, December 22 . . .
Two days until the wedding

How had everything gone so terribly wrong?

Just because he didn't want Casey to take more money out of the business didn't mean he wanted to ruin his brother's life. But that's just what he might have done.

When the police came to question him about the theft of the necklace, Arthur was certain that he himself was on their radar screen as a suspect. A detective asked if the necklace was insured and intimated that Arthur could have stolen it for the cash payout.

Arthur had panicked. "If that's your reasoning, you should be looking at my brother, too. He needs the money even more than I do."

The minute he said it, Arthur hated himself for blurting it out. The detectives had glanced at one another, passing a satisfied look.

What kind of a brother am I?

Arthur was staring into space when there was a knock at his office door.

"Come in," he called.

The electroplating technician entered, holding a slip of paper in his hand. He held it out to Arthur.

"Here are the things we need reordered," he said. "Silver anodes and potassium cyanide."

Chapter 82

Cake flour, baking powder, unsalted butter, sugar, vanilla extract, salt, eggs, whole milk, unsweetened cocoa powder. As Piper lined up her ingredients, she could hear her mother's voice in her mind. *Always have all your ingredients ready before you start.*

Piper took a deep breath and began to make her first wedding cake. Though she had been working on the plans and decoration and preparing all she could in advance, it was only now that it really felt like she was making a wedding cake. She sifted the flour, baking powder, and a pinch of salt in a bowl and set it aside. She cut the butter into tablespoon-size pieces and then beat it until it was soft and creamy. Gradually, she added the sugar, beating until the mixture was light and fluffy. She scraped down the bowl and then mixed in the vanilla.

As she added the eggs one at a time, Piper thought about the wedding. It was still on, at this point, but who knew what would happen in the next two days? Glenna was convinced that Casey was going to be arrested any minute for Jessie's murder. At first, the police thought it was connected somehow to the personal relationship the two had shared, but now, Casey had even been questioned in regard to the diamond theft. The police were speculating that Casey stole the diamond necklace, Jessie saw him do it, and he killed her because of it.

Except for the identity of the perpetrator, Piper thought the police could have that last part right. Piper had seen Jessie rush out of the studio. Maybe Jessie had witnessed the theft and wanted to get away from the thief. But why didn't she tell someone about what she saw, or go to the police? Knowing now that Jessie had written the threatening letters to Glenna, Piper speculated that Jessie wouldn't have wanted to shine any kind of spotlight on herself.

Piper poured the flour mixture, alternately with the milk, into the larger bowl and continued to beat until it was all smooth. Then she divided the batter and stirred the cocoa into a third of it. Piper wet and wrapped baking strips around the pans to keep the cakes level and prevent them from cracking. Finally, she divided the yellow batter between three pans of graduating circumferences, adding the chocolate batter in large spoonfuls in a checkerboard pattern and running a wooden skewer through the batter to create a marbled effect. She smoothed the tops with an offset spatula before sliding them into the oven. Because of their different sizes, Piper had already calculated how long each one would take to bake.

She set the timer and began her wait.

The front of the bakery had a steady stream of customers. Piper helped her mother and Cathy wrap up orders and ring up bills. When there was a lull in the activity, Piper went back to check her cakes.

She inserted a tester into the center of the smallest cake. It came out with just a few crumbs on it. She took the cake from the oven and placed it on a wire rack to cool.

There were a few more minutes until the second layer would be done. Piper decided to use the time to make her daily call to Peggy's parents.

Mrs. Gould answered the phone. "Oh, Piper. Our prayers have been answered. The doctors are going to bring Peggy out of her coma later today."

When all the cakes were baked and cooled, Piper wrapped them well in plastic. She carefully placed them in the walk-in freezer. Freezing them, even overnight, would firm up the crumb and make it easier to level and split.

She heard the little ping come from her BlackBerry, signaling that she had gotten a text message:

PIX READY. WILL BRING 2 WEDDING ON FRIDAY.

Piper moaned. That was two whole days away. She didn't want to wait that long. Piper texted back:

WILL B IN CITY 2NITE. CAN I COME 2 UR PLACE 2 SEE
    THEM?

A few more texts back and forth, and it was settled. Piper would be at Martha Killeen's studio at seven o'clock.

Chapter 83

There was a change of plans.

Piper had hoped to go to the hospital to visit Peggy first, but traffic was backed up from the George Washington Bridge, making her trip into Manhattan almost an hour longer than it should have been. She decided to head straight to Martha's studio, because they had set a specific time. Piper could go to the hospital afterward.

At one point, with cars at a standstill, Piper took out her BlackBerry and posted:

MY FRIEND PEGGY IS BETTER AND MARTHA KILLEEN HAS MY
   PICTURES READY !
SEEING BOTH OF THEM 2NITE !!!

As Piper placed her BlackBerry in the cup holder, she felt a twinge of guilt. She had taken the Oprah Web site pledge to make her car a "No Phone Zone." She knew that that included sitting in traffic. It was just such a hard habit to break.

Once over the bridge, Piper drove her parents' sedan down the West Side Highway, noticing the line of cars on the other side of the divider, going in the opposite direction. The vehicles were barely moving.

Miserable, Piper thought. The idea of the hours all those commuters had to spend at the end of each day slogging back home to New Jersey and Westchester County made her head hurt.

Please, let me never have to do that.

The Fourteenth Street exit led to the old meat-packing district, now the home of designer shops, good restaurants, and trendy bars. Piper turned down Washington Street and made a left on Perry. Miraculously, she found a parking space near Martha Killeen's place.

Piper approached the building, wondering how much something like this actually would cost. Twenty million dollars? Even in a depressed real estate market it had to be worth at least fifteen million.

So close and yet so far.

Chapter 84

He was almost finished. Quent had just one last stack of papers to sort through, and then he finally would be done cleaning out his office.

He picked up the pile and sat on the sofa. He couldn't recall the last time he had been able to sit there. It was always covered with stuff. Stuff that he meant to attend to, stuff that he thought he might need someday.

Quent flipped through the papers, occasionally putting one aside, tossing most in the wastebasket. When he came to the one about cyanide, he stopped. He read the article again, still marveling at the audacity required to kill Travis York in front of so many people.

The days since the murder had been a whirlwind. Going to the funeral, dealing with the police and the press, following Peggy Gould's condition, at the same time revising and rewriting scripts and attending to the final days of shooting in New York City. And then there was the jewelry theft on the last day before moving to Los Angeles. The police had eaten up his time with that, too, wanting to know how it could be related to Jessie Terhune's death.

Quent hadn't liked that woman from the get-go. She was too uptight and prissy. But he certainly didn't wish her dead.

Had all that happened in less than two weeks' time?

Quent looked down at the article on cyanide he held in his hand. He read the date printed on the bottom right-hand corner. December 10. Prompted by the murder, Quent had seen the potential of incorporating a story line about cyanide poisoning into the show. He had done some quick research on the Internet the day after Travis York was killed, and printed it out for future reference.

Chapter 85

The housekeeper welcomed Piper into the entry foyer and asked her to wait while she summoned her boss. Piper remained in the clean, modern space, admiring a large, framed black-and-white photograph hanging on the wall, of a young Asian girl with bangs and big, dark eyes. Piper stepped closer to get a better look.

"My mother took that."

Piper turned to see the little girl in the picture standing near the staircase.

"It's wonderful," Piper said. "Your mother is very talented and you are very pretty."

The child smiled, revealing a missing front tooth. "My name is Ella," she said.

"I'm Piper."

Piper bent down and was shaking the child's hand when Martha came down the stairs.

"Ah, I see you've met my Ella," she said, looking fondly at the child.

"Yes, I was just admiring her picture," said Piper, gesturing to the photograph.

"Well, Ella's going to be late if she doesn't get upstairs and change for the Christmas party at her friend's house."

"I get to stay up late tonight," Ella announced excitedly. "Santa Claus is coming to their house early and we're going to see him."

"He is?" asked Piper. "Well, that sounds like fun."

"Ella's friend and her family are going to be in Europe on Christmas," explained Martha. "The mother thought that since Santa was coming early to their apartment, it would be nice to have a few kids over to enjoy that, too." She turned again to her daughter. "Now, come on, Ella. Get going. Dory will help you change."

Martha's eyes followed the child as she scampered up the steps. "Ella is the best thing I've ever done in my life," she said. "I want to make sure she has everything."

"Well, she sure has it here," said Piper. "This place is fantastic!"

"Would you like a quick tour?" asked Martha.

Piper could hardly wait to look at the photographs but she did want to see the place. She put down her bag and followed Martha up the stairs.

Chapter 86

Alcoholic beverages were prohibited, but one of the guys on the squad had smuggled in some eggnog. For many of the agents, this was the last day of work before Christmas. They had decided to use some of their annual leave to lengthen the holiday. So they were staying a bit later than usual to clean up loose ends before they left.

A desk in the center of the office had become a temporary buffet as plastic glasses, cartons of eggnog, and plates of Christmas cookies made by a few of the guys' wives were laid out. Jack joined the others in some holiday cheer, popping a small cookie in his mouth and getting confectioners' sugar on the lapel of his jacket. He wished he had asked Piper to bring him some of those cookies he liked so much from her mom's bakery.

As more agents gathered, it got noisier. Jack almost didn't hear his phone ringing. He rushed to his desk and answered. It was his N.Y.P.D. contact.

A saleswoman at Saks Fifth Avenue remembered selling the letter opener. Though it had been paid for in cash, sales records showed that it had been purchased less than half an hour before Peggy Gould was stabbed.

Chapter 87

Piper followed as Martha showed her through the home. The kitchen was sleek and spare, with top-of-the-line stainless-steel appliances. The living areas featured glossy wood floors and giant windows to let the light stream through. Finishing that level was a gym, a maid's room, and a powder room. Framed photographs, large and small, were hung artfully on every wall.

On the floor above were the five bedrooms. Two of them shared a bathroom; the other three each had its own. Piper almost swooned as Martha showed her the master bedroom with a massive four-poster shrouded in yards and yards of diaphanous fabric flowing from the ceiling like waterfalls and coming to rest in gentle puddles on the floor at each corner of the bed. The fireplace opposite was the size of a walk-in closet, and the en suite bath featured a sunken whirlpool tub that could seat at least six.

"One more floor, Piper," said Martha. "I think you'll enjoy seeing the lap pool."

As they walked toward the bedroom door, Ella came barreling in.

"Look, Mommy. Don't I look pretty?"

The child twirled around in her red velvet party dress. Piper's mouth dropped as she saw what Ella was wearing around her neck.

Chapter 88

Piper wasn't picking up.

Jack knew from her tweet that Piper was going to visit Peggy. The hospital didn't allow cell phones to be operational inside the building. Piper must have turned hers off.

When the ringing switched to voice mail, Jack left his message.

"Pipe. We've got something on the letter opener. It was purchased at Saks Fifth Avenue with cash. And the salesperson remembers two women. Call me as soon as you get this, Pipe."

Chapter 89

Ella preened, the large diamond necklace glittering against the red velvet.

"I found it in a box in your closet, Mommy. Isn't it beautiful?"

Piper looked at Martha. Their eyes locked, both of them instantly realizing the significance of the moment.

"You can't wear that to see Santa, honey," said Martha calmly. "Let me help you get it off." She took the necklace from the child.

"All right, go ahead now with Dory and have a good time," said Martha. She closed her eyes as she bent down and gave the little girl a long hug. Martha's eyes misted as she watched her daughter run out the door and down the hallway. When the child was out of sight, Martha turned to Piper.

"My God, Martha," gasped Piper. "*You* stole the necklace?"

Martha nodded. "And I'm not proud of it."

"But why?" asked Piper incredulously.

Martha stretched out her arms. "All this is expensive, Piper. I want to give Ella the life she deserves."

Piper's mind made the next connection. "And you killed Jessie Terhune?"

"She saw me, Piper. I had to."

Chapter 90

Two detectives were waiting in the hospital hallway. "You can go in to see her now," said the nurse. "But just for a few minutes."

As the detectives entered the room, Peggy was lying in bed, her head raised slightly, her face colorless. Her elderly parents sat in chairs beside her.

"Ms. Gould," one detective said gently, "can you remember what happened? Do you know who attacked you?"

Peggy slowly nodded once, closing her eyes as she thought of it.

"You recognized the person who stabbed you, Ms. Gould?"

Peggy softly whispered, "Martha Killeen."

Chapter 91

Martha carefully laid the diamond necklace on the tall dresser. In one seamless motion, she pulled open the top drawer, grabbed the gun inside, and turned to face Piper.

"I'm so sorry you had to find out, Piper. I liked you."

"I don't believe you are going to kill me, too," said Piper, terrified but determined not to panic.

"At this point, there's nothing else I can do," Martha said evenly.

"You poisoned Travis, didn't you?" Piper asked.

Martha didn't answer.

"But you might have killed Glenna by mistake," Piper continued.

"It didn't matter to me who died," said Martha, keeping the gun trained on Piper. "As long as I got pictures that I knew I could sell for hundreds of thousands of dollars."

"And Peggy?" asked Piper.

"That was *really* too bad," answered Martha. "She was such a trusting soul, but so naive. Now enough. Get going."

Piper shook her head, yearning for the pepper spray that was in her bag downstairs. "No. If you're going to kill me, you'll have to do it right here and have blood spatter all over the walls. I'm not going to make it easy for you."

"I mean it, Piper," Martha said menacingly. "We're going downstairs to take care of things in the shed out in the garden." She gestured with the gun, pointing it toward the door for just a moment.

That was all the time Piper needed.

Chapter 92

The unmarked police car with the flashing portable beacon barreled down Second Avenue, slowing down a bit at red lights before running through them.

As the detectives' vehicle made a right on Fourteenth Street, the radio dispatcher confirmed that patrol cars were also proceeding to the Perry Street residence of Martha Killeen.

Chapter 93

In a split second, Piper recalled the lessons drilled into her head almost every Saturday morning for years, when her father dragged her to karate class.

The element of surprise is a great weapon.

Legs have the greatest reach and greatest power.

Stay loose, keep your shoulders and arms relaxed.

Breathe, Piper, breathe. Don't hold your breath. Breathing will help you keep your balance.

Be confident. Nothing makes you as slow as indecision and apprehension.

She had done it a thousand times in class, only now she had to do it to save her life. Balancing herself on her right foot, Piper used her hip, knee, and foot, all at the same time, aiming the sole of her left foot at Martha's hand. In a blur, Piper's foot hit its target, sending the gun flying across the room, landing several feet away and skittering across the polished hardwood.

Martha dove to the floor, landing on her stomach. She propelled herself on her elbows, closer and closer to the weapon. In two seconds, her hand was just an inch away from the gun, and Piper leaped on top of Martha's back, arresting her forward motion.

Reaching around Martha's head with both hands, Piper pressed her fingernails into Martha's eyes, pulling her head up and back. Screaming in pain, Martha reached out and blindly wrapped her right hand around the gun. She rolled over on her side, spilling Piper off her back, and shot wildly into the air.

Piper pounced on her attacker again and pinned Martha's left shoulder with her right forearm. She reached Martha's wrist with her left hand and started slamming the photographer's hand against the floor over and over until, in a spasm of pain, it relinquished the gun.

She knew that her next move had to be perfect. Using the side of her left hand, Piper struck Martha's neck in a flash, hitting her just below the ear. The impact to the nerves bundled there rendered the woman instantly unconscious.

Piper heard pounding on the door from downstairs as Martha went limp beneath her.

Epilogue

Thursday, December 23 ...
One day until the wedding

P iper took the defrosted cake layers, covered them
with vanilla buttercream, and then placed them
in the refrigerator for the icing to harden. Taking
out a plastic package of prepared fondant, she put it
into the microwave for just ten seconds, making it
more pliable. She kneaded the fondant ball like bread
dough.

As she misted the bakery worktable with cooking
spray and then sprinkled powdered sugar over it, Piper
gave a silent prayer of thanks that Peggy was all right.
Though Piper hadn't gotten to the hospital the night
before, she had talked with her friend on the telephone.
Peggy's voice sounded weak, but she was totally lucid.
Her doctors were predicting she'd only have to stay at
the hospital a few more days.

As her mother watched, Piper picked up a long rolling pin and began to flatten out the fondant. Eventually she had a big, round shape a quarter-inch-thick. Piper took the cake layers out of the refrigerator and applied a thin layer of piping gel to help the fondant adhere. Then she looped the fondant over her rolling pin, lifted it, and carefully draped it over the first layer. She smoothed, tucked, and then smoothed some more, popping any air bubbles with a pin. Finally, she trimmed off the excess fondant with a pizza cutter.

"You're doing a nice job, Piper," said Terri, her head turned to the side to get a good view. "You don't need me at all."

"I'll always need you, Mom," said Piper. "I don't know what I'd do without you and Dad." She hugged her mother.

Terri beamed. "Did you see how proud he was at breakfast when you told him you used your karate?"

Piper nodded. "Yeah. I don't even want to think what could have happened without it. I'm never going to make fun of his emergency-preparedness obsessions again."

"Never say never," said Terri, smiling. "I have a feeling that your father will go on to bug you another day."

A bell tingled, signaling a customer.

"I'm going to leave you to it," said Terri. "Call me when it's time to stack the layers."

While Terri went to the front of the shop, Piper repeated the process on the other two cake layers and thought about Ella. She wondered what would become of the little girl now that her mother was in custody and faced a life in prison. Dory, the housekeeper, was staying with her for the time being, and it had been mentioned that one of Martha's relatives would take the child. Piper hoped so.

As she stood back and assessed her work, Piper rubbed her calf. It was sore. She had pulled a muscle when she kicked Martha's gun without warming up first.

Two people were dead and another had been through a terrifying ordeal because Martha Killeen had been desperate. Though Martha rationalized that she had committed the crimes for her daughter's sake, Piper wasn't totally buying it. The world-class photographer had become a slave to her possessions and her lifestyle.

Though Piper was thankful for her safety, there was something she would definitely change about last night if she had to do it over again. Instead of going for the tour of Martha's place, Piper wished they first had gone into the photography studio. Vin had talked about the use of potassium cyanide as a reducing agent in labs— maybe she would have seen it in the developing room.

She also would have had the chance to look at her precious photographs. Her dream of having her picture taken by Martha Killeen had come true. She just didn't have any concrete proof of it.

Before she began stacking and decorating the cake, Piper washed her hands, took out her BlackBerry, and texted:

TAKING ON A NEW ROLE: WEDDING CAKE MAKER !!!

A large arrangement of long-stemmed red and white roses was brought up by the doorman. Glenna placed the vase on the round table in the foyer. She took off the cellophane wrapping and smiled as she inhaled the sweet scent of the flowers. Then, she opened the small envelope that was attached.

Her face fell as she recognized Phillip's scrawl.

> *Dear Glenna,*
> *Because of Susannah, I will always be a part of your life.*
>
> > *Phillip*

He had to get in the last word, a parting shot intended to intimidate me and rain on my happiness.

I refuse to let Phillip sour this special time for me.

Glenna tossed the card in the fireplace. There was much to be thankful for, and she didn't want to be distracted from it. Casey was no longer under suspicion. His brother had come to him this morning, apologized for his remarks to the police, and promised to come up with a satisfactory financial agreement.

Tomorrow, she was marrying the man she loved, the man with whom she wanted to spend the rest of her life. Glenna wasn't going to let anybody diminish her joy.

But one thing that she had hoped for wasn't going to happen. Martha Killeen wasn't going to capture the bliss of the bride and groom.

Glenna could live with that.

Friday, December 24 . . .
Wedding Day

Piper, Jack, and ninety-seven other guests watched reverentially as Glenna seemed to float down the sweeping staircase. She wore a flowing ivory gown of cascading ruffles—and a dazzling smile. In front of the fireplace of the grand entrance hall of the Metropolitan School for Girls, before family and friends, she and Casey pledged their love for each other and promised to stay together. No matter what.

After the ceremony, everyone went upstairs for the reception in the old ballroom.

Glenna gasped with delight when she saw the wedding cake with its smooth round layers and glittery stars displayed on a table swathed in tulle.

"Oh, Piper! It's absolutely fabulous!" she exclaimed. "I can't imagine a more perfect cake."

Piper smiled with pleasure. "I'm so happy you're satisfied, Glenna," she said.

"Satisfied? I'm thrilled, Piper. Just thrilled."

As Glenna turned away to greet well-wishers, Jack took a picture of the cake.

"Oh, good idea," exclaimed Piper. "I'm going to post that." Then her face fell.

"What's wrong?" asked Jack.

"I just thought about my Killeen pictures. I wish I could post those, too."

"You can," said Jack.

Piper looked at him quizzically. "What do you mean?"

"I have the photographs at my apartment." He grinned. "You look fantastic in them."

Piper's eyes widened. "You've got to be kidding, Jack. How did you get them?"

"Do me a favor, Pipe. Don't ask."

Piper's Simple Buttercream Icing

4 sticks (2 cups) softened unsalted butter
8 cups sifted confectioners' sugar
1 tablespoon pure vanilla extract

In a large mixing bowl, using an electric mixer, beat the softened butter for 3 minutes. Add the confectioners' sugar, beating slowly. Then add the vanilla and beat on a higher setting until the buttercream is fluffy and very light.

This recipe makes 7 cups of icing. To cover a three-tiered wedding cake, serving 100 people, make the recipe five times.

Acknowledgments

When I was young, my mother made cakes for the neighborhood kids. As each birthday approached, the children perused the Wilton cake-decorating book and picked a favorite. The cakes didn't always turn out exactly like the ones in the pictures, but they were close enough and we were thrilled.

Just as a certain number of eggs or cups of sugar is essential in a cake recipe, there are various ingredients that go into concocting a book. Without the right resources, it would be impossible to come up with a story that hangs together and forms something consumable. Here are the people who added to the first Wedding Cake Mystery:

Always, there is Father Paul Holmes. He offered support, encouragement, creativity, and attention to detail throughout the writing process. Paul embraced the new series, even though wedding cakes are a world away from broadcast news. I appreciate that he was so game and continues to be so loyal.

It took a long time to settle on a title, but Facebook friends Mattie Piela and Linda Rutledge came to the rescue with *To Have and to Kill*. Susan Carroll suggested that a marriage proposal at the Hayden Planetarium would be very romantic. Thank you, ladies.

Research can be delightful. Wilton cake-decorating course instructor Dena Gaglioti taught me how to fashion flowers, shells, hearts, and stars from icing. What fun!

A trip to the New Jersey Library for the Blind and Handicapped led me to wonderful Ottilie Lucas. She is an inspiration. Ottilie guided me as I began to dream up a character with visual impairment. Her reaction to my first chapter on Terri Donovan and macular degeneration encouraged me to go forward.

Lee Cohen, Esq., is the inspiration for Vin Donovan. Like Vin, Lee assembled a beginner's first-aid kit when he was five years old and has been preparing for emergencies ever since. Lee was so generous with his time, sharing his knowledge and experiences as well as coming up with plausible scenarios. He got me thinking about things that I had never really considered before. Lee, you could write your own book!

Elizabeth Higgins Clark helped with Piper Donovan's voice. An actress herself, Elizabeth filled me in, countless times, on theatrical protocol and machinations. She also made sure that Piper sounded like a twenty-seven-year-old and not like the middle-aged woman who developed her. Ah, come to think of it, I developed Elizabeth as well. She's my daughter.

Jennifer Rudolph Walsh and Joni Evans, you both know what you do for me. Thank you, thank you, thank you.

Carrie Feron, Michael Morrison, Liate Stehlik, Lynn Grady, Sharyn Rosenblum, Tessa Woodward, Shawn Nicholls, Bobby Brinson, Virginia Stanley, and the dedicated people at William Morrow/HarperCollins got the series up and running. I know there are so many, unnamed here, who contributed their talents. Please know that I very much appreciate all your hard work.

Finally, my deep gratitude to my readers, for your loyalty over the years . . . and for being willing, now, to give something new a shot.